Hold Me, Cowboy

Wives Wanted:

For all the cowboys of Mule Hollow!

Responsible for helping draw attention to Mule Hollow's national "wives wanted" ad campaign, columnist, Molly Popp's syndicated column is a must read across the country and hopefully her ticket to a reporting job on Times Square.

But lately, she's been featuring ex-bullfighter Bob Jacobs, a reader favorite, more than he's comfortable with and he's just put his booted foot down firm...only turns out he's too late to stop the featured story already coming off the presses. Suddenly Bob-hunting-women are turning up in places they shouldn't be. And when he gets hurt saving one from a rampaging bull Molly must step in to nurse him back to health.

Bob's not happy about the circus Molly has turned his life into and now he's dealing with the sparks that are suddenly heating up between him and Molly, the one woman he's determined not to fall for. Because if there is one thing his past has taught him it's that a reporter will give up anything, even love, if the story or the byline is big enough.

Will love bring these two together?

A Christian Contemporary Western Romance series. Inspirational Novels that will make you smile. Previously published as the Mule Hollow series.

Note: This book was previously published as *Dream a Little Dream*. This edition includes some fun extras.

HOLD ME, COWBOY
Texas Matchmakers Series, Book Four
Enhanced Edition

DEBRA CLOPTON

Hold Me, Cwboy
Copyright © 2017 Debra Clopton Parks

This book is a work of fiction. Names and characters are of the author's imagination or are used fictitiously. Any resemblance to an actual person, living or dead, is entirely coincidental.

No part of this publication may be reproduced, distributed or transmitted in any form or by any means, including photocopying, recording, or other electronic or mechanical methods, without the prior written permission of the publisher, except in the case of brief quotations embodied in critical reviews and certain other noncommercial uses permitted by copyright law. For permission requests, please contact the author the author through her website: www.debraclopton.com

CHAPTER ONE

Molly Popp noted that the cattle guard in front of her was like a giant billboard proclaiming in bold letters NO TRESPASSING, and yet, she was about to cross it anyway.

If she wanted a picture of the house that sat a hundred yards from the road—and she did—then she needed to cross this cattle guard, drive through the herd of bored-looking black cows and top the hill that left only the red rooftop visible from where she sat. Piece of cake.

She told herself Bob Jacobs, the owner, wouldn't mind. After all, this was a win-win situation. Then why did she feel she was about to do something she was going to regret? She'd never used photos before, but her editor thought a picture would add a new touch to her popular weekly newspaper column. And he'd thought

Bob's ranch would be a good image to start with...especially since he believed readers would be very interested in the ranch after her column came out tomorrow.

Gripping the steering wheel of her convertible VW Bug, she told herself to relax. But it actually wasn't just the picture that was bothering her.

It was tomorrow's column.

Had she stepped over a boundary with it? Remember, win-win, mutually beneficial.

"Yeah, yeah..." she sighed, and tried to calm the churning pit that used to be her stomach.

Just do it, Molly! This is a good thing.

Reaching for her camera, she dipped her head through the strap, and made certain it was turned on, since there was no need to waste time once she was there—after all, this was a surprise.

That's right! It's a surprise, so perk up, Molly, and do this, think positive.

On that note, reassured somewhat, Molly pressed the gas and in a teeth-jarring instant shot across the row of steel bars of the cattle guard. Hair whipping in the wind, dust flying behind her, she guided her little Bug as it sped up the gravel road toward the crest of the hill. This *was* for Bob's own good!

She hadn't made it twenty yards when the formerly

slow-moving, bored-looking cows in the field suddenly started trotting toward her, converging on the road ahead of her and surrounding her on all sides! It was as if she was the magnet and they were paper clips. Not wanting to hit the animals, she was forced to switch from gas to brake and within seconds she was at a complete standstill surrounded by the big curious bovines.

"Shoo!" she called weakly. This was not in the plan. Not the plan at all. It occurred to her too late that a topless car might not be the best thing when one was encircled by a group of cows. But she didn't know what to expect from cows. She was a city girl and she'd just bought her new VW convertible because her friend Lacy had a convertible and seemed to have a lot of fun in it.

She'd never thought about *drool*. But there it was, dripping over her front hood from an all-too-inquisitive cow. "Shoo! Shoo!" she called a bit more strongly. "Go away."

The herd just looked at her with eyes that said, *yeah right*. One cow started rubbing its side against her passenger door and another one joined in slobbering on the car. "Yuck!" she exclaimed, as yet another one licked her window then started to nibble on her windshield wiper. "Aw man, that's just not right—"

In reflex she honked her horn. So much for surprise. But she couldn't let them eat her car. To her dismay they didn't run from the blast of her horn. As a matter of fact they suddenly came closer. It dawned her as one stuck its head into the backseat that maybe a horn was used to call them to dinner. Hadn't she seen that somewhere?

When one started to place its head between her and the steering wheel, she screamed—to which the cow suddenly threw its head back and vamoosed away from the car.

Okay then! Maybe that was the way to get something done. She opened her mouth to scream again but stopped when she heard the low rumble of thunder and saw cattle parting, as if they'd been struck by lightning. And then she saw it wasn't thunder she'd heard as her attention was drawn to a fast moving object barreling through the path between the parting cows.

One minute Molly was sitting behind the wheel of her car and the next instant she was scrambling to get into the passenger seat as the biggest, blackest humpbacked bull charged straight into her car door! Just ran into it like a runaway train!

The impact threw Molly into the air and her camera hit her in the chin, which she barely even noticed. She was too busy screaming!

HOLD ME, COWBOY

The crazed mass of writhing muscle slammed into her car again and again while, heart in her throat, Molly clung to the headrest and struggled to get a grip of the terror threatening to immobilize her. When the car lifted on two wheels, she realized the road was built up from the ground slightly. The car was at a precarious disadvantage—toppling over from the leverage and power behind the bull's colossal bashing was almost unavoidable. When it bounced back onto four wheels she knew she was going to have to make a run for it or chance getting squashed if it flipped.

The thought had just clicked into place when Bob's white truck blasted over the top of the hill and raced in her direction. It was a sight Molly would never forget.

She was saved, she thought.

However, the raging bull swung its massive head to the side and glared at the intruder and to Molly's dismay pawed the earth, spun toward the truck, then charged. Unable to believe that the bull would take on the huge truck, Molly sprang to her feet to stand in the seat. She was totally unprepared when in a flash the crazy animal changed its mind, whirled back around and attacked her car again. Molly sailed backward. Flipped like a pancake right out of the car, she hit the ground with a thud. The wind whooshed right out of her and she figured she was a dead duck.

"Sylvester!"

The shout was music to her ears as she struggled to stand, then slipped on a wet cow patty and almost went down again. Bob Jacobs sprang from his white truck, Indiana Jones to her rescue, whip cracking above his head—the answer to her prayers. Was he ever!

Like the rodeo bullfighter he'd once been, the gorgeous cowboy was in his element, charging the startled brute. "Sylvester, get out of there. Move on!" His command was as sharp as the crack of the whip he wielded with such skill.

Molly relaxed a little, still standing in the bull's sights but reassured by the authority in Bob's voice and the steel in his eyes. He was a beautiful sight to see, working the whip around, letting it explode once more just above Sylvester's head.

Mild-mannered Bob is a hero!

Her hero.

Suddenly adrenaline pumped through her veins like water churning over Niagara Falls. Modern-day Knight to the Rescue! The headline flashed across her brain, bumping the shock out of the way and driving her to react. This was good. Really good! Instantly the reporter in her took over and, despite the danger, she lifted her camera and started snapping shots.

Watching Bob in action through the viewfinder of

her camera proved she'd been right all along. She'd known the first day she'd arrived in Mule Hollow and watched him carry hay bales down Main Street that he was the kind of man dreams were made of. Once she'd come to know him, she realized it was true in more ways than just his good looks. The easygoing cowboy had a heart as big as Texas.

And he was going to make her dreams come true.

The belligerent bull snorted and swung toward her, a menacing glare in its eyes—*Retraction*—Bob was going to make her dreams come true *after* he finished saving her life!

Sylvester had literally trampled Molly's tiny car and, as Bob flung himself between the irresponsible reporter and the unpredictable animal, he thanked the Lord for looking out for those without sense enough to look out for themselves.

"Put that camera away," he shouted, unable to believe she was taking pictures! On the other hand, he couldn't remember seeing her without her camera except during church on Sunday, or when she had her laptop or pen in her hand. The woman was always working on a story.

Her reply was to snap some close-ups of him.

Reporters! Disgusted, he grabbed her arm and pressed her behind him. "Back toward the truck. Now," he demanded. "Sylvester's not finished, he's only deciding what he's going to stomp next—you, me or the car again."

At last, letting the camera swing from the strap around her neck, she locked her hands around his biceps, cutting off all circulation she squeezed so tightly.

"I thought you knew him!" she gasped. "I thought you could control him. I mean, he listens to you, right?"

Her breath brushed his ear as she stretched to her tiptoes behind him, her camera digging into his back. "I *own* him. Big difference." He angled his arm behind him, pressed his hand to her side and directed her toward his truck, keeping his eyes glued to Sylvester, his whip ready for action. "Believe me, when a two-thousand-pound animal goes into a rage no one controls him if he doesn't want to be controlled."

"C'mon just back up, nice and slow," he urged, instinctively wanting to reassure her. She nodded against his shoulder. Her hands moved to his waist clutching like vise grips, and her chin dug into his shoulder as she stood on tiptoe watching Sylvester. They'd almost made it without stumbling over each other when Sylvester lowered his head, turned back toward the poor car and charged again.

The impact was so unforgiving that the animal and car both lifted from the ground for a solid second. The sound rocketed through the air like an explosion.

"You have *got* to be kidding me!" Molly cried, springing toward the animal like a wildcat protecting her cubs she bolted past him.

"*Oh no,* you don't," Bob said, scooping her around the waist and hauling her back.

"Let me go!" she elbowed him in the ribs.

"Ouch," he grunted again when her heel hit him in the shin. "I'm not going to let you commit suicide. Not after all the trouble I just went through to save you."

"But my car!" She waved toward the calamity.

Still clutching her around the waist, he spun them both around and lifted her through the open door of his truck and shoved the struggling woman inside. Behind them the crushing sounds of Sylvester battering her car reverberated through the air, a reminder of what could have happened to Molly. Thanking the Lord again, he climbed in behind her, tossed his whip to the dash and grabbed the gearshift.

"Wh-what are you doing?" She pointed past him, her fingers fluttering in front of his nose as she sputtered.

"I'm getting you out of here." He paused, glancing at her for the first time as he pressed the gas pedal.

"But you can't. My car! What about my car?" She yanked her hand back and glared at him with huge eyes.

"Sylvester's not finished with your car. And right now all I care about is keeping you safe and letting him calm down. What were you doing in my pasture anyway?"

They'd reached the cattle guard only twenty feet from where Molly had met Sylvester. She twisted onto her knees in the leather seat to watch her car take another hit through the back window. "But," she gasped weakly, latching onto his shoulder again.

"That's all I can do at the moment." He felt bad for her. "Its only a car. You should be glad it's not you out there getting plastered."

She met his gaze and in the same movement lifted her camera and started snapping shots through the back glass.

What a breed! Reporters never ceased to amaze him—it was always about the story. And yet, he'd seen the terror in her eyes, knew she was coping on her own terms.

He still didn't like it.

At the road, she finally stopped clicking pictures and slumped into the seat facing forward, her foot tapping a rapid beat on the floor mat. She was no doubt figuring all the different ways she could twist this story to meet several papers', magazine and blog formats at one time. She should be in shock, but no, it was the story that obviously had her mind whirring!

The next few miles were ridden in silence. Bob struggled to calm down before saying anything else he might regret. From the corner of his eye he studied Molly.

Molly Popp.

He'd noticed her the first day she'd driven into Mule Hollow several months back. He'd been helping set up Main Street for the town fair when she stepped out of her car and sent his world spinning.

Who wouldn't have noticed her? She had long chestnut hair that shimmered in the sunshine with every purposeful step she took. Today it was pulled back into a ponytail, a few strands fluttering around her face, drawing attention to the wide green eyes that dominated her delicate features.

Those had been his first impressions of the beauty at his side. She was a nice person. A stunning woman. But it hadn't taken long to realize she wasn't the woman for him. He'd momentarily forgotten she was a reporter. A fact that emerged after only a few conversations with her. There was no missing the sparkle in her eyes as she talked about her work. It was clear that Molly's career was first and foremost in her mind—which was her prerogative. But he'd stepped back quicker than a cowboy hearing the rattle of a Texas rattlesnake.

His prerogative was to look for a wife. He wasn't interested in playing the field and dating for the sake of dating. He wanted to settle down with a traditional woman—a wife who would focus on him, the children they would have and the life they would build together. Yep, Bob might have rescued Molly because she needed rescuing—and he couldn't help but enjoy looking at her—but he knew where to draw the line on his emotions. For months, that line had been drawn right there on the ground in front of Molly Popp. *Reporter.*

But there was one problem that had steadily gotten worse over the past few weeks.

Molly had decided to use him as a step toward achieving her goal.

And that wasn't going to happen.

He'd been putting off confronting her about mentioning him so much in her weekly column. However, finding her in his pasture was the last straw. It was time to talk.

"Why would you have a killer bull in the pasture in front of your house?"

"What?" Her words sliced through the silence that

had built between them like an arrow toward a bull's-eye. He focused and met her accusing gaze. "I don't normally." The woman had some nerve. He'd give her a little slack because she'd been traumatized by his bull. The thought of what that maniac would have done to her if he hadn't heard the sound of her horn plagued him. But the fact of the matter remained that it was none of her business what his animals did on his private property.

Still he found himself explaining.

"Sylvester broke through a gate this morning and headed straight for his girlfriends. I had one of my other bulls in there while he was recovering from an injured hoof and it was driving him mad. Clint Matlock and J.P. were on their way to help me corral him."

"Corral him? He needs to be shot."

Bob arched an eyebrow at her and her expression crumpled into remorse.

"Okay, maybe not shot. I'm upset. But he needs to be put far away from people. He's an animal. And I mean a *wild* animal. He just charged me! Right there out of the blue. I mean I didn't even see him coming! And his girlfriends, they *tricked* me. They were meandering across the road. I think they were doing it on purpose. I really do. To distract me and get me to stop. And then *wham!*"

She was talking faster than an auctioneer. The earlier terror in her eyes was replaced with anger. Even though she'd been in the wrong for trespassing on his land, thus endangering her life, Bob still felt a sense of guilt at her unfortunate morning.

But she'd been trespassing on his private property. Just as she'd been trespassing on his life with her newspaper articles.

He pushed the truth aside and tried to focus on getting her to town and out of his truck before he said something he might regret.

He thought about how this woman would do anything for a story. Her actions proved it. "You were taking pictures—"

"Excuse me?" she huffed. "I figured if I was going down I should go out with a story. I mean, when I was trapped inside the car thinking I was about to get killed, I could just see the humiliating headlines. You know the ones that would read, *Reporter Molly Popp Found Squashed Like a Bug Inside Her VW Bug*. Nope, I refused to go out that way."

He glanced from the road back to her. "Everything with you is about a story. Do you ever just relax and enjoy the day without thinking about the next idea? The next angle? It's not healthy."

HOLD ME, COWBOY

He looked back at the road. Her grunt of disapproval told him he'd stepped on her toes. This wasn't the first time they'd had this discussion. Not long after she'd come to town they'd gotten into it, lightly. It had started out as a quiet discussion they'd had one night after church. And like now, they'd agreed to disagree.

It was the reason he'd known not to pursue the undeniable attraction he felt toward Molly.

And he *was* attracted, but competing with a camera and a computer were not his hopes and dreams for his life. Molly's mind never ceased looking for an angle. And he had no plans to live every day with that kind of mind. Or everyday "agreeing to disagree."

Through no choice of his own, Bob had been down that dead end road once and he wasn't about to go there again. *Ever*. No matter how much it had bothered him to shut down his interest in Molly.

Which brought him full circle with the little matter that needed to be resolved between them…her using him as her main story in the world of good press. Apparently the woman would crawl over anybody to keep her precious name in the paper. It was disgusting. Her syndicated column was about Mule Hollow, and everyone who lived there, but somehow, slowly, he'd become an increasing headliner.

"What are you going to do about my car?"

Her changing the subject wasn't a surprise. She never wanted to talk about her inability to join in with the real world. He took the opportunity to try and back off from the agitation building inside him. He tried instead to focus on the right way to handle this, not his gut reaction.

"I'll have Prudy come over as soon as we get Sylvester out of there and he can take it back to town. I'll call my insurance agent first thing in the morning." He glanced at her. "I am sorry about your car."

And he was, but it was time to get a handle on the situation. This showdown had been building for weeks, a showdown he prayed about and thought would be resolved for him. But clearly the Lord had decided to leave the fixing up to him. And he couldn't ignore it any longer. Bucking up his resolve, he directed the big truck toward the side of the road. This was not something to discuss while driving. He slid the gear into Park and turned toward Molly.

"What are you doing?" she asked, swinging toward him, surprise written in her reaction.

Bob shook his head, amazed at her ability to seem so naive. The best thing for him to do before he chickened out and let those big mossy eyes work on him was to get right to the heart of the matter. "Why are you writing about me so much in your column?"

She blinked. "I write about everyone."

"Not like you do me. And why are you snooping around my house? I've had it, Molly." He rubbed his temple, trying to focus on his agenda. "It's bad enough you're writing about my personal life for all the world to see, I don't need you putting pictures of me in there, too. Matter of fact, that's what this is about. I don't want you writing about me anymore. Got that?" There, that should do it.

She could go her way and he could go his. And maybe the nagging interest he was continually needing to redirect away from her would vanish once and for all.

CHAPTER TWO

Okay, so maybe she deserved the accusatory scorn that she saw in his eyes. To an extent. Molly raked a hand through her hair, remembering it was in a ponytail only after her fingers snagged against the beaded scrunchy. He'd just told her not to write about him anymore!

"What have I written about you that's so terrible? I've only generalized about what a nice guy you are. Just like I do about all the cowboys in Mule Hollow."

He snorted in disbelief, his dark eyes narrowing as the color changed from navy to almost black like a cloud darkening open water.

"Are you joking? I'm showing up in the papers more than the President. I can read, you know. And even if I couldn't, everybody in Mule Hollow gets a real treat quoting me every line you've written about me. Enough already." He took off his straw Stetson and held it between his tanned hands only to stuff it right back over his curls and lock his jaw.

He was really mad. Molly had never seen Bob mad. The guy was the mildest mannered man she'd ever met, which was one of the many qualities that had attracted her to him in the first place. But this was ridiculous.

"Seriously, what have I done that is all that bad? Tell me."

"Cassie." He nailed her with frank eyes.

"*Cassie?* I can't believe you're mad about Cassie! She's a sweet girl. You made a great impression on her."

"I like Cassie. But she stalked me for a month if you remember!"

"Hey, most men would love to have a beautiful young woman chasing after them. And besides, I did hear you say, right there in Sam's Diner, that you'd specifically bought your own ranch so that you would be ready when the Lord sent you a wife. You said that you were going to step out on faith and show the Lord you knew He had someone special out there for you. You said you were going to settle down and get prepared."

Bob frowned and yanked his hat off again. Those distracting dark curls drew her attention once more until his navy eyes slammed into hers. "I said that to Clint Matlock in confidence. You were eaves-dropping—"

"Eavesdropping! Are you kidding! You were sitting in Sam's Diner. Everyone heard you say it."

"That may be true." He gritted the words through barely moving lips. "Still," he snapped, on a second wind, an angry wind, "it doesn't give you the right to think you can plunk me in the middle of your stories like a poster boy for some Lonely Cowboys Foundation. Come on Molly, I said I was getting ready for the wife *God* was going to send me. What makes you think God needs your help? Because I certainly don't."

Heat suffused her face. "Now that's not fair. God's using me."

"And *you're* using *me.*"

That tripped her up for a moment. True, her column had been picked off the wire by a huge number of newspapers across the country. The interest in what was happening in Mule Hollow was a phenomenon!

Though she'd already gained some praise and recognition for one of her personal segment articles prior to moving to town, it had been her reporting on the Mule Hollow phenomenon that had put her on the map. Everyone was interested in the dying little town that had done a national ad campaign for wannabe wives.

Even magazines that never had given her the time of day were suddenly interested in what she had to say—on the subject of Mule Hollow as well as other topics. It was a dream come true and she couldn't deny it.

Of course, in the big world of media Molly realized only her pinky toe was in the door and the overnight recognition could be gone in a flash. But to say that she was *using* him...well, it sounded so wrong.

"It's a win-win situation," she said in her defense. "I get the recognition I need to move up in my career while you and the other fellas get invaluable exposure that will lead would-be wives to our little town. I'm helping you fulfill your dream."

He hitched a brow giving him a bit of a rakish look and her heart began the familiar jig...the Bob jig, as she referred to it.

The guy didn't even know the effect he had on women, which was part of his appeal. He wasn't a spotlight kind of man. He was a little shy about all the recognition he was getting. That was what the fuss was really about, she reassured herself.

"You know my work is helping Mule Hollow. There's life in town now, when only months ago the place was drying up. Why the fact that Adela, Norma Sue, and Esther Mae put in motion this plan to revive their beloved town has won over the country's interest. I'm just reporting on the influx of husband-hunting women coming to answer the call."

It was true, even if his scowl said he disagreed. Molly was meant to be here. Her help was crucial. The fact that her articles had caused a young woman like Cassie, without home or family, to hitchhike to Mule Hollow in the hope of finding what she'd never had...thinking of the young woman brought tears to Molly's eyes.

For her, it had been Lacy Brown—now Lacy Matlock—who'd inspired her to move to the town and change her life.

The wacky hairdresser had recognized her mission in life when she'd read the first ad and instantly moved to Mule Hollow to open her salon and help bring life to the town. She'd believed, and rightly so, that the women would read the ads about a bunch of lonesome cowboys and that they would come. And she'd believed they would want to look good while trying to find the right cowboy. But most important, she believed that while they were getting all spruced up in her salon, she would be able to witness to them.

And it was happening. Molly had been the first person Lacy had talked to about the Lord. That conversation had changed her life.

HOLD ME, COWBOY

Molly had accepted the Lord into her life and begun to build a personal relationship with Him that very day. She was stumbling all the way, but trying, as Lacy had shown her by example, to put God first in everything she did. Not an easy thing to do. Especially when someone like Bob didn't fully appreciate the good she was striving to accomplish.

The man *had* said he wanted a wife. She was simply trying to help him!

And she wouldn't do that for all the bachelors. Oh no, some of these cowboys were lonesome for good reasons! No ambition, partying all the time, not an ounce of respect for a lady...but the ones like Bob—*especially Bob*—were wonderful guys and she only wanted to help.

Her thoughts whirring, she met his dubious stare straight on, his denial ringing in her ears. He might not think he needed her help, but God had called her to Mule Hollow for a reason. Maybe at first coming to the quaint little town had been about career strategy, but that had lasted about a week. She had started seeing things differently the instant the Lord entered her heart.

Women out there needed *good* men. Decent men.

And that fundamental realization had set off a lightbulb in her brain. It didn't take long to see Mule Hollow was packed full of wonderful, God-loving men. And like Lacy kept telling her, God had His reasons for bringing her here. What better reason than to use her talents to showcase the good guys? Lead the women to water, as Norma Sue was fond of saying. So that was what she was doing before she moved on to her next step up the ladder of success. She'd been showcasing all the cowboys. She couldn't help it that readers loved Bob.

"Well," Bob said, bringing her wandering brain back to the present. "God might be using you, but, like I said, I'm not in need of your services. The conversation I had with Clint was none of your business."

She expelled a slow breath, fighting the urge to glare at him. "I'm only trying to help," she reiterated, starting to feel nervous. Really nervous.

He met and held her gaze with one that said he disagreed. She narrowed her eyes, refusing to back down. She couldn't. She truly hadn't done anything wrong. Had she?

His eyes narrowed to mirror hers then suddenly the skin where his dimple would appear if he smiled started quivering, as if it was going to give way and turn into a smile at any moment. Molly breathed a sigh of relief. She just might be off the hook.

"Look Molly, really, I know you haven't meant any harm. I know you *think* you're helping me, and you're certainly helping Mule Hollow. There is no denying that it's been put on the map through your articles. But I'm done. I want out. Do you understand?" He dropped his chin to his chest then looked straight at her.

Molly's throat went dry and she tried to swallow the lump that had lodged there. The acid in her stomach attacked the inner walls as she tried to digest Bob's words.

No way around it. Her boat had a hole in it.

Bob engaged the gears and guided the truck back onto the road. When he started whistling softly to himself, Molly blinked and started fidgeting with a loose thread on the seam of her jeans. That was Bob. The good-hearted guy who was going to make some lucky woman a wonderful husband was back to being himself again. Just like that, he'd forgiven her for what he thought was an intrusion on his life.

Just like that, he thought all was well, everything fixed.

Molly struggled to breathe, watching the brightly colored town appear on the horizon. She didn't feel the jolt of happiness she normally felt upon seeing it set there welcoming her. As brightly variegated as a box of crayons, just as Lacy had intended when she talked the town into painting the dull, dry, clapboard buildings, it should have brought a smile to Molly's lips.

Not today.

Her thoughts were riveted to the article she'd submitted earlier in the week.

The one her editor had requested because of overwhelming reader interest...the one that hit the streets tomorrow. The one that was too late to retract. The one she'd meant for good...really.

CHAPTER THREE

The aroma of strong coffee, thick bacon and Sam's unbelievably seasoned eggs were enough to make a good cowboy buckle with hunger. What man would miss home cooking when he could get something this fantastic by just walking in the door of Sam's?

Call him crazy, but Bob could. Not that he'd ever had that much home cooking…but he missed it. Longed for it.

It was a simple fact that no matter how much he enjoyed the food and company at Sam's, Bob wanted more. He wanted a home, a family. He'd wanted it all his life. Being raised in a boarding school did that to a guy. He pushed aside the old anger at his dad for choosing his career in journalism over him. But even though he'd forgiven his father, it hadn't changed the fact that he longed for the family bond he'd never had since he'd lost his mom at an early age.

Fond memories of how life had been before her death drove him to want more now.

And after years of planning, he'd decided it was time he put his faith into action and show the Lord he believed He was going to send him the perfect wife. And so he'd taken the step forward and bought his ranch just a month earlier.

It had been a big step for him to change the timetable on his long-term goals. His life had been going pretty close to the target he'd set for himself back when he'd quit the pro bull-riding circuit and taken the job working for Clint.

He had set goals but realized he hadn't left any room for faith in those plans.

After watching his buddies fall in love and get married when they'd least expected it— and be so happy as a result—he'd realized maybe he needed have a little more faith.

He took a seat at Sam's counter, Of course faith and letting Molly continue to use him for her own career advancement did not mix.

She'd dodged a bullet yesterday when he'd managed to keep her from being maimed or killed by Sylvester. What had she been thinking?

She'd been a thorn in his side for weeks. Ever since

the Cassie incident. The girl had hitchhiked to town because of Molly's articles just to marry him...or so she thought.

And Molly didn't think she'd done anything wrong by sticking him in those articles so much. After putting his foot down yesterday maybe life could resume on an even note. Molly could do her thing and he could do his. There would no longer be any connection between them, which was a good thing.

So everything should be fine...right? Right, except he'd had an uneasy feeling ever since he woke this morning.

Sam burst through the kitchen's double doors, drawing his mind back from the sudden nagging sense of discontent. "Mornin', good-looking," Sam chirped.

Bob eyed the dinner owner. "What'd you say?"

Flashing an unusually bright grin, Sam set a coffee mug in front of him and poured his stout black brew into it. "Now don't go bein' all shy, you handsome hunk of a man," he drawled.

Lately everyone had noticed Sam had been slightly distracted and grumpy. But this was just plain abnormal. Bob was about to ask if his longtime friend was feeling okay but the diner's door swung open and the morning crowd of hungry cowboys stampeded inside. His friend and ex-boss, rancher Clint Matlock, was in the lead.

"Well hello, *Bob*." Clint lifted an eyebrow and punctuated the word *Bob*. Another abnormality for the morning.

"Hey, handsome!" someone called.

"Honey doll, could I have a date? Purdy please," came another squeal.

Bob swiveled in his seat toward them as more catcalls followed. His heart sank. One of the cowboys was grinning at him like a lovesick cow batting his eyes, while another slid across the floor on one knee and grabbed his hand. Bob yanked free before the cowpoke's puckered lips could plant a fake kiss on it.

"Hey! Watch out!" He glared at them with a withering sense of dread. This was not good. Not good at all. Bob groaned, watching in dismay as they collapsed with laughter and fell over on each other in total glee. At *his* expense. Cowboys picked on each other for one reason and one reason only. To rub something in. But *what?* Bob swung back to his coffee, racking his brain.

What had he done to bring on this kind of ribbing?

Until someone let him in on the joke he'd ignore them. Grabbing his coffee, he took a drink as if he couldn't hear the laughing and backslapping going on behind him.

HOLD ME, COWBOY

His coffee was in midair when Clint slid the morning's paper across the counter in front of him.

The black-and-white pages were folded neatly to Molly's column, *About Town in Mule Hollow*. In bold black letters the headline read: He's The One You Need.

Bob choked on his coffee when his name jumped off the page at him. Everything going on around him faded away as he read the words. Suddenly the burning sensation in the pit of his stomach had nothing to do with hot coffee.

"I guess you didn't read the paper this morning," Clint drawled.

Bob met his friend's gaze, the corners of his lips twitching with barely contained laughter.

"She didn't..." was all Bob could manage, as his stomach knotted with fury.

Clint placed a hand on his shoulder. "I'm afraid she did. *Handsome.*"

"He's the one you need," Lacy Matlock read from her styling chair at Heavenly Inspirations Hair Salon. She paused and looked at Molly over the top of the paper before continuing. "Not just any cowboy, handsome Bob Jacobs has a heart of gold and would make any woman an excellent husband. He's so sure that God is going to send the right woman his way that he's stepping out on faith...."

With mounting dread Molly watched Lacy's eyes widen. The unease that had clung to her all night squeezed tighter around her middle. If only she'd known how Bob felt last week. Instead of yesterday. If only she'd known how he felt before it was too late...

She'd hardly slept a wink last night before she'd finally risen early, called Lacy at home and asked her to meet her down at the shop. Preferably before her Saturday morning appointments started arriving. Knowing that Saturdays were the day when the majority of cowboys came in for cuts, Molly wanted to be in and out before any of them saw her. Cowboys were early risers and by daylight they'd all have had their morning coffee and read the paper. And after having just reread it herself, in the light of what Bob had dictated to her yesterday, things were about to get tense.

Tense-ha! He was going to kill her.

Normally her column was simply her somewhat witty dialogue on the goings-on of the endearing town and all of its residents—the cowboy population most specifically. But this was different. This write-up focused totally on Bob. By reader demand! She had to remember that part.

"Does Bob know you did this?" Lacy asked, rolling up the paper and swatting the table with it, grinning. She was actually excited! An excited Lacy Matlock meant proceed with caution, there were sure to be curves ahead.

Molly hadn't expected Lacy's excitement. She closed her eyes and shook her head. "No. Not yet."

"Oh boy."

That didn't sound encouraging. Molly nervously rolled her pencil on the tabletop with her pointer finger, trying not to grab it and run. "He said he wanted a wife. He said it in the diner for anybody to hear." Why was she defending herself? What good would it do? "So I felt obliged to help," she tagged on the end, imploring Lacy to reassure her that what she'd done was perfectly natural and acceptable.

Not, Lacy's laugh said instead. Her blond hair jiggled she laughed so hard.

Molly straightened in her chair and felt herself grow pink. "Lacy, it's not that bad. C'mon."

Lacy waved her hands in front of her face as she struggled to gain control of her laughter. "Molly, Molly, Molly. Don't kid yourself. This article is fantastic. If I wasn't already married and living in Mule Hollow with my very own dreamboat, I'd have packed my bags and headed this way the second I finished reading this. Who could resist Bob? I mean, you make him sound like the best thing since…since chocolate! That man's going to be dodging women left and right."

Molly tugged at her ear and chewed on the pencil eraser then yanked it out of her mouth when part of it crumbled on her tongue. "Do you think it will be that bad?" Jumping up she grabbed a tissue from the manicure table and spit the bitter eraser into it.

Lacy rolled her eyes and drummed her pink fingernails on the table, a trait of hers that was sure to leave lasting impressions on all hard surfaces she encountered. Between her eraser spitting and Lacy's incessant tapping, they had a regular concerto going on, a musical of impending doom.

"Molly, your very words are…" She paused, snapped the paper open and cleared her throat obnoxiously. "'Bob, with his to-die-for dimples, thoughtful wholesomeness, mixed with just the right amount of charm, might be enough to make this Mule Hollow lonesome cowboy the perfect husband, but it's his faith in the Lord that sets him ahead of the game.'" She pinned Molly with eyes as bright as topaz. "The women are coming, girl. Believe it. Just a few mentions of him in your columns were enough to bring Cassie out here to try and marry the guy. Or had you forgotten?"

Fat chance. Molly's stomach churned, and her hand drifted to toy with the simple gold chain she wore around her neck. "I'll admit I did get a little carried away. I might have gone a bit overboard."

"No! Are you kidding? It's all true," Lacy exclaimed. "Every last word. But, girlfriend, my question to you is, if you noticed all of that, why are you advertising him? Why aren't you signing up for the position as Mrs. Bob Jacobs?"

Molly took a step back and shook her head vigorously. "Nope. Don't go there. You know good and well, Lacy, that I didn't come here to marry."

Lacy dropped her jaw a notch. "I know you are just like I was. You came for your career, and now you are doing one humdinger of a job getting the word out about the single cowboys here just yearning for true love. God's given you a path and, honey, you are just blazing down it full speed ahead. But...and I mean this with all the love of a good friend, *you* not marrying—well that's a bunch of hogwash, as Esther Mae would say."

"Hey, that isn't very nice."

Lacy popped up, waving her arms wide. "You love it here Molly. You might be dreaming that writing for some fancy newspaper in some giant city is where you want to be, or crawling through some jungle, but I can see in your heart that Mule Hollow is in your blood now. Maybe when you first came here you thought you wanted to be somewhere more exotic, but after a few months here you're now one of us. All you have to do is admit it."

Molly pushed away the voice in her head that wanted to agree with Lacy, the part of her that longed to relax and put her roots deep in the Texas soil that surrounded this minuscule tad of a town. But she couldn't.

She'd had a plan, a dream, for most of her life. You didn't just chuck a lifetime dream out the window when it was finally within your grasp.

Besides, Bob Jacobs might be the best-looking man she'd ever seen and her heart might go pitter-patter every time he stepped near, but that didn't mean anything other than the fact that she knew how to appreciate a good man when she saw one. And that was that. She didn't tell Lacy any of the last thought, though.

She wasn't insane. Instead, she argued the facts. "Lacy, forget me and Bob. Our life goals are aeon's apart. Bob wants a *Leave It To Beaver* June Cleaver type, or a Martha Stewart—minus the criminal record—wannabe. Ha! Those icons would be the last two people on earth I would ever be confused with. Nor do I have any desire to emulate them." Well, that wasn't exactly the truth...it wasn't that she didn't have hopes of conquering the kitchen—she did. But so far her Tuesday night cooking classes hadn't turned out so well. She was actually dangerous in the kitchen.

But even if she were to master cooking beyond her trademark lasagna with canned sauce, never, ever would there be hope for her to become a domesticated diva. "I need to go, Lace. I'm supposed to meet with Bob's insurance agent down at Prudy's place first thing this morning. Speaking of which, have you seen my car?"

"Have I seen it! Girl, Norma Sue came hurling herself into the diner last night talking about how terrible Sylvester had destroyed it. I'm telling you, Molly, Clint said it was only by the grace of God that you weren't hurt. Thank goodness Bob showed up when he did. That bull is a maniac when he's been away from his pasture for a while."

"Then why do they keep him around?"

"Because he's a champion. And he only gets crazy at certain times. Clint says Bob has made a mint off that bull. Believe me, him escaping from his pasture was more of a mistake than just the fact that he could have killed you. People pay really good money for Sylvester's offspring. Clint said the first and best investment Bob made was Sylvester. The bull financed his new ranch and enabled him to buy the other bulls that he owns."

"Are you serious?"

"Oh yeah. Clint said buying that particular bull was an act of genius on Bob's part. He's just a little high-strung."

"*Mean* is more like it," Molly grumbled as she said goodbye, poked her pencil behind her ear, slung her backpack to her shoulder and headed toward her car—or what was left of her car.

It was a hard walk. She had to force every step. Because of that bull she'd had nightmares. The last place she wanted to go was to see the destroyed car that could very well have been the end for her. Sure, while it was going on she'd been able to disconnect herself from the danger. She'd actually taken pictures of Bob as he raced to save her life! How crazy was that? *Who* did something like that?

The man must think her an absolute loony tune. But at the moment, she was thinking the same thing about him. Here she was trying to help him find a wife and he had this bull problem. And it wasn't anything to pooh-pooh away. Didn't he understand, great investment or not, if that crazy bull killed someone, he was going to have a hard time finding a wife from behind bars?

HOLD ME, COWBOY

Rounding the corner of Prudy's Garage, she came face-to-face with her mangled car, and her knees almost buckled at the sight of it. Her mouth went dry and her palms grew damp—it was as if she were back in that moment. She could feel the car shaking as Sylvester slammed into it. She could see the solid wall of pure bull muscle bunching and rippling. Feel the car tilt and start to roll. She winced. The toast she'd forced down for breakfast suddenly threatened to revolt and, covering her mouth with her trembling hand, she whirled away. On shaking legs, she stumbled back to the street, praying for the Lord to help her keep her breakfast down.

If the diner had been a fiasco, the feed store was a circus. Applegate Thornton and Stanley Orr were hunkered over their endless game of checkers, a mixture of the *Odd Couple, Grumpy Old Men* and *Mayberry*. The two old-timers, who normally played checkers down at Sam's Diner every morning at daylight had recently moved their game to the feed store. It had been a surprise to everyone. Applegate, Stanley and Sam went way back with one another and now to have this rift between them was just plain confusing. Something had happened two weeks ago and no one had been able to figure it out. Or get any of them to talk about it. To Pete's sorrow, they still weren't on speaking terms with their old buddy Sam, a fact they made everyone aware of on a regular basis because, though hard to believe they could get any grumpier, they were like grumpy old men on spinach.

However, they were still in touch with their newspaper. Something Bob found out the instant he stepped through the door to purchase feed.

"Bob," Applegate shouted. As usual, his hearing aid was off. "Says here you're out to get married. Who's the woman?"

"Come on, Bob," Stanley added when Bob didn't respond. "It's all right there in the paper. Next thang ya know one of them gossip magazines is gonna have Bob's picture plastered across it. Like a hunk of the month or somp-thin."

Bob spun toward the two men. "Applegate, my picture isn't going to be in any kind of magazine. This'll be old news tomorrow." If he could only be so lucky.

"I don't know about that, son," Stanley said, scratching his bushy eyebrow, his wrinkled face drooping with a doubtful expression. "My cousin's son's barber's grandson's friend had himself a little *sit-chi-ation* involving a dead body in his backyard and before you could blink, it was on the cover of the *Inquirer*. Right smack on the front. You remember that, App?"

"Huh?" Applegate shouted. "I thought that was yer sister'-n-law's, brother's, ex-stepmother'n-law's father?

"Hey, guys." Bob held out his hands to halt the mind-spinning deluge, holding on to his temper as best he could. This was getting more ridiculous by the second. "I won't be on the cover of any magazine. Thankfully I don't have the same connections your friend had."

Stanley shot him a glare of disbelief. "He wasn't my friend! The twerp ended up going to prison. Turned out he killed the feller. Them magazines, they get it right ever once in a while—though I ain't of the mind that Elvis is alive. That one I'll have to see for myself."

"You say Elvis is alive?" Applegate asked, having totally misunderstood what was being said. "Why, that's about the all-fired most foolish—"

Pete showed up with Bob's order on the dolly, and he didn't slow down as he wheeled it outside. Bob wasted no time following.

"I'm telling you, Bob, if those two don't get over this feud they have going on with Sam, *I'm* going to go mad! If it's not one thing it's another. I've about had all the—well, you don't need to hear about my problems. I read the paper, too, and it looks like you have enough on your plate."

Bob started stacking the heavy bags onto his truck.

"I feel for you, Pete. At least I can load this up and hop in my truck and go home. If you don't see me for a month or so you know where to find me."

Pete, a large man, dusted his hands on the front of his well-filled shirt. "You really fixin' to hole up at your place for that long?"

"*I wish*. If I could I would. Believe me, there's plenty to keep me busy, the place was pretty rundown when I bought it. So I imagine I'll be back and forth." He paused and glanced at Pete. "Truth is, I'm about ready to commit a murder myself. This is just not right, Pete. You should have seen the fellas down at Sam's. As long as I'm around, I'll never live this down. I mean, how could she have said all that, that flowery stuff? The woman is trying to make a name for herself writing about all us cowboys and she's clueless about how the boys take stuff like that and run with it."

"Oh, son, I feel your pain," Pete laughed, slapped him on the shoulder then headed back inside to his own problems. Bob slammed his tailgate shut and paused to take a calming breath. That's when he saw her. She was coming around the edge of Prudy's Garage, greener than the snake she was.

Without another thought, he struck out down the middle of Main Street, his spurs clinking with every step.

It was time for a showdown.

CHAPTER FOUR

The familiar sound of clinking spurs drew Molly's attention away from almost upchucking in the middle of Mule Hollow's Main Street. The sight of mild-mannered Bob storming toward her sent a shiver down her spine.

The blaze in his eyes meant only one thing. He'd read the article.

Retraction. There was nothing mild mannered about the man storming toward her.

She swallowed hard, sucking in a calming breath.

It was time to face the music.

Bob halted three feet in front of her, legs spread shoulder-width apart and planted his hands on his narrow hips. If he'd been wearing a Western duster, she could envision him sliding the coat back behind the gun holster, his fingertips wiggling just above the pearly, white pistol, itching to draw and shoot.

Get a grip, Molly.

"H-hello, Bob." She lifted her chin, trying not to look as queasy as she felt.

He lifted his chin in acknowledgment, or challenge, his eyes boring into hers. The man did have the nicest square chin and the most stunning eyes…angry eyes at the moment, but gorgeous. And why was she thinking about them, when he was obviously thinking about wringing her neck? "I, well I was just looking at my car. It's a mess." She laughed nervously as he raised an eyebrow. "Okay, okay." She raked a trembling hand through her ponytail. "I see you've read the article. I'm sorry. I should have asked. I should have made certain that something like that, I mean, an entire article about you should have had your okay on it."

He nodded. That's all. Just a curt nod and nothing. Except that his eyes kind of glinted in the morning sunlight like a ping. An "and you call yourself a reporter" kind of ping.

"But," she rattled on, "you said it and, and well, my editor had asked me to do an article that focused solely on you." He lifted his eyebrow and guilt washed over her but she stumbled on. "It's what a poll of the female readers said they wanted. I started not to do it. Really, but then I overheard you talking to Clint. I mean, really, there I was sitting in Sam's minding my own business and you just happened to be sitting in the booth right behind me, talking about wanting a wife." She was rambling. There was nothing pretty about rambling, but how else to tell the tale? She just hoped he'd understand. She smiled nervously.

He *wasn't* smiling, so her smile melted like a deflating balloon into a pathetic shriveled pucker. "And well, I think you get the rest of the idea. It was just too coincidental to pass up. How was I to know you were about to tell me not to talk about you at all in my articles? I'm sorry. It was already on the presses," she finished weakly.

Even though she knew she looked as if she'd just eaten a lemon, still he said nothing, just looked at her. *Looked at her,* and she felt even worse than she'd felt.... "All right, already, would you say *something!*"

"Something."

Oh! Molly felt her eyes go squinty of their own accord. So *now* he wanted to be cute! Ooh...she felt like the lowest of low and he wanted to be cute! Fumes were wafting from her ears, she could feel them. She hoped he could see them.

"Look, Molly, I think you've learned your lesson."

Learned my lesson! And she had tried to apologize to the man! She crossed her arms and glared at the rude cowboy.

"I know I've learned mine," he continued smoothly.

Her mouth fell open and a huff escaped before she could snatch it back.

He lifted an eyebrow. "I learned, if you're anywhere in the room I'll keep my mouth shut. It really wasn't your fault. I mean, look at you. You have a pencil stuck behind your ear and a camera strapped around your neck. And I bet inside that backpack there's a couple of notepads crammed full of ideas you've gotten between now and the time you woke up this morning. Hey, you may even have your laptop in there. I mean you wouldn't want to go off without your precious tools."

Molly glowered more. He thought he knew her so well.

"I'm right, aren't I?" he said, tipping his Stetson back a bit with his thumb.

"No."

He smiled and her heart did a weird little sputter. His smile bloomed, showing his dimples, and his midnight blue eyes flared. "I *am* right, aren't I? How many story ideas have you had since you woke up? Let's see, you told me once that you woke up at five every morning because you were the most creative at that hour, and now it's nine. So you've had a few hours of free time…

how about five ideas?"

Molly swung away from him. Here she'd thought he was a nice cowboy. He was just a smart aleck. It was a good thing she didn't have a stick, or she would have whacked him with it! Without a backward glance, she strode down the street toward her apartment. Ooh! If she had a car she'd have made an explosive exit and driven away, leaving the maddening man in her dust. Choking.

"So how close am I?" he asked beside her ear, his warm breath feathering along her neck.

She jumped and swatted at him with alternating hands. How dare he follow her that close. She could feel him smiling. Gloating.

He stepped up beside her. She glanced mutinously at him, increasing her pace. A lot of good it did her—his legs were longer than hers. She paused—where had she been going? Oh yes, her apartment. Focusing, she started walking again. Faster. She could feel her thick ponytail swinging back and forth with every step she took.

"Come on, Molly, let me see the notepads. You've been up writing away as fast as your little fingers can fly. Who're you picking on this week?"

Molly slammed to a halt and twisted to face him. Her ponytail slapped her in the face. "Okay!" She pushed strands of hair off her nose so he could see that she was glaring at him. "Okay! You've had your fun. You've made your point. Now go. Go away. Disappear. Shoo." He was standing tall and lean. His powerful shoulders were squared and his handsome head tilted just enough to show off his triumphant grin and those dangerous dimples. Those mind-boggling dimples that made him look like country star Joe Nichols's long-lost twin, especially when mixed with his twinkling eyes. It made Molly want to…well, she wanted to—

He reached and took the pencil from behind her ear. "Don't write another word about me." Sliding her pencil behind his perfect ear, he spun on his heel and walked away. Strolled away down Main Street with a clink and a swagger.

And her pencil.

Molly's hands were fisted tightly—the man was not the person she'd thought he was. Nope. There wasn't a nice bone in his strong, lean body.

Bob rubbed his new pup's tummy, watching as the little fella grinned up at him with no worries in the world. He was a cute little border collie that Bob had been waiting to pick up from its owner for the past six weeks. After having his little run in with Molly he'd swung by for John Boy.

Patting the pup's rump, Bob sent him scampering to play with a clump of long grass as he went back to work. Tugging his gloves back on, he glared up at the blaring sun and wiped the sweat off his brow with the back of his forearm. He'd been working like a maniac to strengthen the ancient barn that had seemed on its last legs when he bought the place. Bob wanted to make it hang in a while longer. So he was repairing it, using it to clear out his frustrations.

J.P. had offered to help him; Bob had declined. He'd needed the physical exertion. Needed time to think about what had happened that morning.

He'd been pretty hard on Molly.

He'd told himself she deserved his sarcasm, but he wasn't sure he hadn't gone too far. There was a fine line between anger and downright meanness. The truth was, he'd acted like a spoiled bully.

Because of it, here he was thinking of skipping church. The thought made him feel worse. But he wasn't ready to face Molly or the Lord. *Like you can hide from Him.*

Of course he wasn't fooling himself. He could feel the Lord watching him, feel that gentle whisper on the wind. Nope, there was no getting away from Him.

But Molly.

Well, that was a different story. When a guy sang in the choir like he did, there was no way to escape people. The congregation stared up at the choir members as if they were an alien species or something. Not *everyone,* but half of them. Applegate Thornton's dour face came to mind, making him cringe.

But aside from that, he knew Molly would try her best to ignore him, and he would try his best to ignore her. But their efforts would be in vain, because in the long run sometime during the service they would lock eyes and he would feel compelled to apologize.

And frankly, he wasn't ready.

He'd let her off easy before. Not this time. Hoisting a one-by-six in place, he pulled his hammer from his tool belt, a nail from between his lips and in two steady swings drilled the nail into the board. He'd been right! Despite feeling bad about the bull attack he'd had completely legitimate reasons to be angry at Molly.

She'd been out of line. "You're doggone right she'd been out of line. Way out," he said to the wind.

Still. There was the part of him that had come out a little harder than he'd planned. He wasn't completely comfortable about that.

And then there was that other thing—the part of him that kept thinking about how sweet she looked standing there all decked out in her reporter paraphernalia. Despite every reason he had to be turned off by that part of her, he always seemed to conjure up pictures of her looking cute and sassy with the chewed-up, pink-tipped pencil sticking out from behind her ear. But that wasn't what was bothering him right now, either. Something had been wrong with her when he'd first glimpsed her coming around the corner of Prudy's Garage. She'd looked sick.

She'd looked shaken. She'd looked green. And he'd not cared in the least.

Now that bothered him. He'd wanted to make her feel as bad as he could so he'd worked on her guilt and ground it in. He had ignored the fact that the woman had been through a very harrowing experience. A bull the size of Sylvester was a terrifying sight from afar. Up close and personal, out-of-his-head angry like he'd been, Sylvester could tear through a person and never stop. As a rodeo bullfighter, Bob had seen plenty of bull riders mangled by the animals—he'd been there a time or two himself. In those situations the bulls were only doing their jobs. Bull riders wanted a good ride. A mean ride. The better the bucking, the higher the score.

What had Molly been thinking? She could have lost her life all for a picture of his house. He knew facing a mountain of solid bull muscle just by crossing a cattle guard wouldn't have been a priority on her list of things to do for the day. Surely she'd seen the big brute? Who could miss two thousand pounds of bull out in broad daylight? Or maybe Sylvester had been standing over the hill where she couldn't see him.

He wondered if she was having nightmares. Though she'd seemed fine on the ride into town after he'd rescued her, he wondered. Sometimes adrenaline got a person through a close call. Lowering his hammer, he let his gaze wonder out across his pastureland.

A Christian man, no, *any* kind of man worth his salt, Christian or not, would step up and see if she was okay.

Especially the man who knew he had a bull with problems.

Before church on Sunday morning Molly was sitting in her apartment lost in thought.

After her maddening encounter with Bob the brute on Saturday, she'd met with his insurance adjuster alone. He had given her an assessment of the damage to her poor darling car. Her little Bug had taken a beating from that *bull-headed* bull on the hood and both side panels. The adjuster had assured her the news was good, that Sylvester's damage was actually minimal. Some new doors, a little bodywork, a new paint job and her car would be as good as new.

Easy for him to say. New paint jobs were never as good as the factory. Everybody knew that, but it served her right for trespassing. What had she been thinking?

About a story.

Everything in her life was about a story. It was true, but she liked it that way. Still, it seemed a sad fact that she'd stood in the middle of the street taking pictures of her car as it was being towed away that day. But the photos were for "just in case." Just in case she got over her fright and an idea for a story should arise from this incident. That was the way she was wired. Many would argue that her wires were really messed up.

Who was she kidding? She felt no real desire to look for an article angle. Looking at the car had brought all the trauma of the experience back to her. She sucked in a long breath and forced the thoughts away. She refused to think any more about the bull attack. She couldn't. She had just a few days left to get her column in for the week, not to mention the magazine articles that loomed in a consecutive wave of deadlines. She'd scrapped the follow-up on Bob and now she had nothing.

Nothing.

For a girl with endless ideas, the fact that she had no desire to write was unbelievable. She always wrote, had always created several ideas at once.

Specifically, she'd been writing columns about Mule Hollow for almost a year. Now suddenly for the first time in her life she was drawing blanks.

She hadn't had an idea since the attack on Friday—the day Bob told her to stop writing about him.

For the past two mornings, as she'd done most mornings since her arrival in Mule Hollow, she'd risen at five o'clock, dressed quickly, strapped on her backpack and jogged to the edge of town. She'd taken the well-worn path she'd created across the open field where town gatherings were held, past the grove of mesquite trees and finally stopping at her special spot—a flat rock on the top of a knoll overlooking a sweeping valley. There she'd sit. She loved watching the sunrise, bringing with it inspirations—the sparks that ignited her creative mind.

Until now.

Until she'd been given the order to halt all tales of Bob.

She hadn't completely realized exactly how much her column about Mule Hollow had truly revolved around him.

Why was that?

This morning, after not sleeping most of the night, she had sat on the floor in the middle of her apartment surrounded by weeks and months of copies of her column. And lo and behold, to her surprise, the maddening man had been right.

Completely, unexplainably right.

He *had* been in the papers more than the President!

CHAPTER FIVE

Monday morning came and Molly remained distracted and disgruntled, still drawing blanks. Even at church the day before she'd been in a fog, unable to focus on the service. Especially when there was a noticeable vacant spot in the choir where Bob usually sang. The man had a voice like Tim McGraw and he used it for the Lord. Wow! Just one more big check mark for why he was such a great guy. But it still didn't explain why he'd appeared in her articles so much. There was, after all, an entire town full of great guys sitting in the church sanctuary. True, their voices weren't as good as Bob's, but they were nice guys looking for love. So why hadn't she plastered their names all over her articles as much as she'd plastered Bob's? Still boggled in the brain and running late on her routine, she crossed the street and walked over to the tiny Mule Hollow convention center to see if she needed to lend a hand before finding somewhere to settle and try to write. The center was really two older buildings on Main Street that the town had renovated into one large space. By city standards it was nothing more than a big room. For Mule Hollow, it was a convention center. Today they were decorating for Dottie Hart and Sheriff Brady's bridal shower on Friday. The wedding was less than two weeks away, and as far as the two of them were concerned, that was two weeks too long.

An inspiring story, Molly was pleased to have had a hand in the match. It was her articles that basically inspired Cassie to start hitchhiking her way to Mule Hollow, which led Dottie to give her a lift, which brought both of them to town. Dottie had met Sheriff Brady and the rest was history. The only bad part for Molly was that Cassie had followed Bob around. *Followed,* not *stalked* as Bob had called it. And though things hadn't worked out between them, Bob had befriended the young girl and now there were no hard feelings. At least not between Bob and Cassie. Obviously, the same didn't go for her and Bob.

Still, she didn't quite get it. He was happy for Brady and Dottie, he was friends with Cassie. But he was angry with her for writing the articles that were responsible for the wonderfully romantic web that God had used to get them all together.

True, she'd gone overboard expounding on Bob's worthiness as a potential husband, but she'd done a good thing for everyone else.

She was sorry she'd given him more fame than he wanted. But he would live. And maybe God would use it for good. If she focused on the positive aspects of what she'd done, then maybe she could get past this momentary stumble her creative mind was going through. Taking time out this morning from her usual routine to help decorate for the shower would be a good way to relieve the stress that was blocking her flow. It could also provide fodder for the story she would write about the upcoming wedding. Readers were eating up the happily-ever-after wedding stories.

"Molly," Lacy sang from her perch on the top of a twelve foot ladder. "Just the woman I need. Sheri just jogged over and told me I have a walk-in waiting on me for a color repair. Can you finish tacking these streamers up? As soon as I fix whatever this woman has done to her hair I'll be back. Although Sheri said this was a job for a magician not a beautician so it may take a while."

"And who says you aren't a magician?" Esther Mae called out from her chair in the center of the room.

"Yeah," added Norma Sue with a snort. "Anybody who saw Esther Mae's red triple decker before you got a hold of her would know you've got some great tricks up those sleeves of yours."

Esther Mae harrumphed and Norma Sue gave her an innocent look. "Hey, I'm still waiting for it to go poof and turn back into the pumpkin that it was."

Lacy laughed and climbed down off the ladder. Spinning around toward the two older friends, she plopped her hands on her hips. "You two better straighten up and be nice to each other or I might just have to get my razor hold of y'all."

"Hey," Esther Mae snapped, her eyes growing wide. "How do you think I would look with one of those spunky short cuts? You know where my hair sticks up on top of my head—"

"Lacy," Norma Sue broke in. "Don't listen to her. Mule Hollow doesn't need to give the wrong impression."

"And just what does that mean?" Esther Mae gasped indignantly.

Norma Sue dropped her jaw. "You'd look like a red-headed troll! That's what."

Esther Mae blew out a short breath. "Pooh. I would be spunky and cute. Just like my personality."

Lacy shot a wink Molly's way. "You are right about

the personality, Esther dear. But I think maybe we'd have to have a serious consult before I punked out your hair. Okay, I gotta go."

Molly watched Lacy jog toward the door, chuckling. "What do I need to do?" she called after her, not at all sure about attempting decorating without a whole lot of instruction.

"Oh!" Lacy spun at the door. "As Esther Mae and Norma Sue get those decorations done, all you have to do is string them like I did these." She pointed to the ceiling where she'd been draping the lights and ribbons Norma Sue and Esther Mae were braiding together. "Don't look so doubtful, Molly. You can do this. The ties are on top of the ladder. As soon as I can, I'll be back. If I'm not back before you get finished, you'll know either I've got a really, really bad disaster on my hands or I'm getting to tell whomever is over there waiting on me about the Lord!"

She grinned, her eyes sparking with excitement. Everyone knew that witnessing for the Lord was the reason Lacy woke up every day. Molly had experienced it firsthand in the middle of a highlight.

Taking in Lacy's beautiful work, Molly realized there was no way her streamers were going to remotely resemble the artfully draping decorations her friend had strung. Every dip was perfectly matched, no bulges, no kinks. Molly plastered on a smile and thought positive. "Sure, I can handle this, Lacy. You go do that thing you do."

"Catch ya later," Lacy sang. "'Bye, Norma Sue and Esther Mae. Try to be good, why don't ya."

"Hey, what fun would that be?" Norma Sue laughed, studying her work. "Don't you agree, Molly?"

"Oh yeah. Sure thing." She raised an eyebrow at the two spicy women. Picking up a strand Lacy had already strung across the floor, she climbed the ladder, listening to the two friends chatter on, returning to their previous banter without skipping a beat.

"What would possess you to think about cutting your hair like that?" Norma Sue asked.

Esther Mae gave an exasperated sigh. "I feel fat. I thought maybe a shorter cut might help."

"Esther, it doesn't work that way!"

"Well, something has to give. I tell you I can't fit into my dress," she wailed. "The wedding's two weeks away and I'm as bloated as a cow. I think Sam gave me the wrong prescription. I've been taking my new derivatives and all they're doing is sending me trotting—"

"Pulleeze!" Norma's hand shot up. "Skip the trotting part. And the word is *diuretics!* And why are you blaming Sam?"

Esther harrumphed. "The sign does read Sam's Diner and *Pharmacy*. And, he has been acting weird lately is all I'm saying. He's even being rude. And you know Sam—he might be grumpy sometimes but not rude and distracted. I'm telling you something's up."

"Maybe he's just being cranky for no reason—it happens sometimes. Or maybe he isn't getting enough sleep," Molly offered.

"Well, he's been that way for days—I think he's thinking about Adela. I think something is wrong. Haven't you noticed the food at the diner hasn't been up to snuff lately?

Norma Sue nodded and stopped braiding. "Now that you mention it, Adela has been extra quiet lately." Molly thought about that. Everyone could tell there was something special between Adela and Sam. But there seemed to be an invisible line drawn between them. They always sat beside each other at church, Sam making certain Miss Adela was comfortable after she came down from playing the piano, fussing over her sweater when it fell off her shoulders as she sat down. It was the sweetest thing Molly had ever seen. It was one of the things that made Molly have some hope about—well, she wasn't going to think about that right now. She had too many other things pressing to be worried about why Sam wouldn't ask Adela to marry him. "Maybe we need to do something," Esther Mae snapped, sitting up straighter and drawing Molly back to their conversation.

"Oh no, you don't."

"Norma Sue, you know those two are in love. They need our help. Tell her, Molly. Tell her it's our duty to make sure Adela and Sam see the writing on the wall."

"But I—" Molly felt trapped as she stared at the wall and willed herself to be invisible. She was already in enough trouble for messing with Bob's life. She didn't want Sam and Adela mad at her, too. They seemed to have things under control.

"Yeah, Molly," Norma Sue chimed in. "Maybe Esther Mae has a point."

"I...well." Molly scrambled down the ladder and grabbed her backpack from where she'd set it by the door. "Look. I just remembered something I forgot to do. Y'all can figure this out on your own. Do whatever you feel you need to do."

Feeling guilty about abandoning the job, she backed out the door and closed it before she could hear their startled replies. She was still too shaken up over Bob being so put out with her. She wasn't cut out for all this matchmaking any more than she was cut out to be a decorator.

She was a reporter. She was supposed to stand back

and record what was going on around her. To document it in a professional, even creative way was something she strove hard to do. But she'd never experienced anyone being upset with her work, and she wasn't sure how she felt about that. Not sure at all.

As a matter of fact, Bob's displeasure had brought up a whole cache of hidden questions she didn't want to think about right now.

She needed to write.

She needed to write and not think about anything other than the words on the paper.

And that pretty much summed up how she'd always looked at life. Until lately, when the words refused to flow.

It was nearly eleven o'clock as Molly hoisted her backpack to her shoulder and started to cross Main Street. She paused, thinking about poor unsuspecting Sam and Adela. Norma Sue and Esther Mae's snooping might be just what they needed to take that next step toward the altar—it had worked many times before. But Molly had never actually had a hands-on experience in matchmaking. Sure she had written some articles that expanded on the original ad campaign that Adela, Norma Sue and Esther Mae had started with.

But she had never point-blank picked two people and set out to manipulate them to fall in love.

Then again, that wasn't really what was happening at all, not exactly. No one could *make* a couple fall in love, not even the matchmaking pros of Mule Hollow. There had to be that special connection. "Sparks," as the ladies were fond of calling it—and they were hawks at spotting those romantic little embers. And it made them happy. And she was happy for them if that was what they wanted to do. She, on the other hand, was content to simply write her articles. She certainly didn't have the knack for seeing sparks of a romantic nature. Now sparks of a disturbing nature—that just might be her niche!

What was happening to Bob was as close to getting involved on a personal level as she'd ever gotten. That was a really sad thing if she let herself dwell on it. She had a problem with closeness. But really, with the life she had chosen, closeness wasn't a factor.

She stepped off the plank sidewalk and started across Main Street. At the sound of a fast approaching vehicle, she glanced over her shoulder, jumping out of the way just in time for a gray minivan to whiz past her. There was nothing like nearly getting creamed to make a person lose her train of thought. Molly's mouth fell open in a silent scream as she glimpsed the driver looking over her shoulder talking, completely unaware she'd almost mowed someone down.

Molly's heart was pounding at the near miss. She couldn't move for a few moments, trying to collect her wits, but her eyes were glued to the disappearing van of death.

She didn't recognize it so she assumed it was from out of town. At the end of the street, at Prudy's Garage, the brake lights came on and the vehicle careened to a halt beside the gas pump. It had no sooner stopped moving than suddenly heads popped out of every window! From this distance Molly thought it looked like the van literally exploded with kids. Five at least. No make that six...*seven!*

She was counting, when the driver stepped from the vehicle in her spandex-looking black pants and her four-inch red heels.

Oh my. That didn't look like a mother of seven. Molly immediately wondered what her story was? Her imagination started chugging, drawing her toward Prudy's. Stranger in town. Car full of kids. Was it by accident? Was she a woman looking for a cowboy?

There certainly could be a story in this, despite the bad headline. As Molly drew closer, the woman leaned back into the van and pulled out what looked suspiciously like a cake. A pound cake. Yes, from this distance she thought it looked like a pound cake settled on a square of foil-covered cardboard, wrapped with pink transparent plastic wrap. She squinted in the sunlight and could see a purple square in the center, like a name tag.

Was there a cake sale going on somewhere Molly didn't know about? Maybe there was a fundraiser going on? No, she would have known if there was a fundraiser. That was her job to know these things.

Prudy ambled out of the grease bay squinting at the woman through his oil-speckled glasses. Molly racked her brain, making mental notes as she tugged her pencil from behind her ear and pulled her emergency notepad from her back pocket. Nearing Prudy's, she heard the woman ask a question. Molly knew it was a question, because all of a sudden Prudy's greasy hands began to move and wave and gesture. Everyone knew Gordon P. Rudy—Prudy for short—talked with his hands. It was fairly entertaining. And since Mule Hollow was such a small place, a person needed all the entertaining they could get. The problem was that most of the time Molly didn't understand Prudy's sign language!

Nobody did.

So there she was, pencil poised, paper in hand, only to watch as her story sashayed back to her van, yelled at the kids to buckle up, then sped off.

Okay, so maybe there wasn't a story there. Prudy, obviously not heartbroken or in love, scratched his head and ambled back into the building without giving the disappearing van a second look.

Molly paused. It left her to wonder whether she was so desperate for a story that she'd begun to imagine leads. What was so unique about what had just happened? Honestly nothing. She was just desperate.

Arrggghhh! She stomped her foot, rammed the pencil back behind her ear and contemplated her situation. She had to get over this. She had to move on, and she would. Her well wouldn't stay dry without a fight. Serious reporters didn't let a thing like this get in their way. They didn't freeze up because of...because of... because of what? She didn't even know what to call what had happened to her.

Stuffing the notepad back into her pocket, she abandoned the rest of her walk to Prudy's. How hopeless was she, that she was going to try to write a story out of a woman asking for directions? Head wagging, she made it across the street, beelining toward her special rock. But first she needed coffee.

A big cup. The nastier the better to hit the spot. Turning on her toe, she detoured to Sam's. Sam's trademark coffee was dark and caustic, and had on occasions supercharged her brain after a late night of writing. Today she just needed a jolt. She had definitely not been doing any writing!

And besides, after what Norma Sue and Esther Mae had said, she thought she needed to check up on Sam. Maybe something *was* wrong. Maybe he needed a friend. He *had* seemed out of sorts lately.

"How do, Molly," he greeted her as soon as she pushed open the door. "The usual?"

She plodded to the counter, letting her backpack slide off her shoulder onto the stool, suddenly feeling drained. Glancing around the old-fashioned diner, it was an odd thing not to see Applegate and Stanley playing their daily game of checkers by the window. But at the moment she was glad the place was empty. Maybe she could get Sam to talk. She was, after all, a reporter and that was what she did. Right? "Hi, Sam. Do you have any old coffee this morning? Maybe some that you forgot to take off the burner last night. Some that's as thick as mud and stronger than bootstraps."

Sam frowned, wiped his hands on his white apron and reached for a cup. "That bad, huh."

She nodded. "'Fraid so." She hated to be so glum. Especially since she was here to find out about him. Why had he seemed so moody lately? It hit her that maybe it was because of Applegate and Stanley moving to Pete's.

She watched him pour coffee into a large paper cup for her. He'd ordered the paper cups especially for her so she could take her coffee to the woods and write. "Sam, are you feeling okay? Is something bothering you?" There. She'd sliced right to the root. Sam was, as far as Molly was concerned, the sweetest man on earth, even though he hid it under an endearingly gruff exterior.

"Just peachy," he said. "Don't you be worrying yer pretty little head about me none. Worry about poor Bob. You need to give one of them cowboys some newsprint time other than Bob. That cowboy's had all the ribbin' he can take, Molly girl."

The acid in Molly's stomach churned up once more. "Did they tease him terribly?"

"Now, Molly, you know how these cowboys are. 'Fraid I did it, too." He looked repentant, but only momentarily.

Molly slapped her hand on the counter. "You should be ashamed of yourselves!"

"Ashamed of what? That's the way men are. You gave 'em ammo and they used it. Don't you go athinking Bob wouldn't do it, too—well, now that I think about it, Bob just might be the one guy who wouldn't do it. But that's neither here nor there. They was just havin' a peep of fun and he'll get over it. But you still need to focus on somebody else. Now go get to work. Mule Hollow needs you, so stop lollygagging around here."

Hiding a smile, Molly shouldered her pack and backed toward the door. "That's why I came by, not for the turpentine you call coffee, but for your abuse. Sets me straight every time. I love you anyway."

And she did. She and Sam had a connection. They teased each other always and loved every minute of it. It was another one of the things that connected her to Mule Hollow. Sam was like a father figure to her.

Of course he didn't know that. No one did. Until Lacy Matlock had introduced her to the Lord, Molly hadn't felt connected to anyone. Because of her own father's indifference to her, she'd stopped seeking personal connections with people early in her life. What she hadn't gotten at home she hadn't sought out elsewhere. She'd wondered sometimes if something in her was broken, but she didn't worry too much about it. Some people just had a bad home life, and she was one of them. Besides, she was a reporter with an agenda aiming for bigger things. Each story she wrote was a specific notch upward toward achieving her goals. Making her dreams come true.

Dreams she'd been dreaming...for years. Those dreams had held her together when life at home threatened to break her apart. A Houston businessman, her dad had been hard to live with. She could still hear the fights—fights that had driven her to hide in her closet, the way a child attempts to drown out the constant turmoil. It had been her imagination that saved her. Dreaming of the world that lay outside the boundaries of her small tumultuous existence had helped her cope.

Mule Hollow, though she loved it dearly, and though it represented more of a home to her than anything she'd ever known growing up, was still just a stopping point. She would leave it behind when the time was right.

She dreamed of being overseas, writing for one of the five respected magazines or newspapers she'd set her mind on. She knew if she just kept working her plan, she could achieve her dream. Her time was near. She'd garnered some interest and sent out résumés and felt confident her break was about to come.

But she hadn't meant to hurt Bob in the process of making her dreams come true. Sweet, wonderful Bob. The cowboys at Sam's had probably been horrible.

No wonder he'd been so upset with her. So curt and so unlike himself.

Still. The man had said specifically that he wanted a wife. She hadn't gotten that fact wrong and she hadn't written anything hurtful. Sure, he'd been teased, but would he hold that against her when he found Miss Right?

Molly thought not. Despite her worries, if she helped him find his one true love, Molly felt he would be so happy with her that he'd give her a big ol' kiss for helping him!

Not that the kiss she was thinking he'd be giving her would be anything like the kind he would give Miss Right.

Molly frowned as she stepped off the sidewalk. For a bizarre minute there she'd imagined the other kiss, the one reserved for the woman of his dreams.

The loud roar of an engine interrupted her runaway thoughts. She was grateful for the interruption. Turning around, she watched as a powerful purple-and-chrome motorcycle pulled to a stop in front of the diner. It was an unusually busy day for Mule Hollow. Counting the walk-in at Lacy's, this made three out-of-town visitors today. And it wasn't even the weekend.

That was really peculiar.

But then, what hadn't been strange about the past few days?

CHAPTER SIX

Bob spotted the van before he pulled across the cattle guard on his way into town for more nails. It was parked beside his mailbox. The windows were rolled down and there were little kids hanging out every window. There was a woman standing beside the driver's door waving at him.

Thinking she must be having car trouble, he parked, hopped from the truck and jogged over to offer his assistance.

"Ma'am, can I help you?"

She patted her fluffy orange hair and rubbed her hands down the front of her tight black pants—at least he thought they were pants. They were so snug they could have been skin.

"Hi, *you're* Bob," she said.

By the way she was blinking, Bob thought maybe

something was in one of her eyes. And her voice sounded funny, like maybe she had a cold, all hoarse and deep. And she talked real slow.

"I can *tell* by the dark curls and dimples." She drawled out the word "tell" with a dramatic Southern accent.

Bob took a step back, wondering how she knew who he was? He hadn't shown her his dimples. They only showed up when he smiled. And he wasn't smiling right now. He couldn't very well deny who he was, even though he had a really bad feeling about what was to come. He tipped his hat to her, it was the mannerly thing to do. "Yes, ma'am. I'm Bob. Do I know you?"

She smiled a giant red smile and her eyes went to fluttering like she was about to take flight. He did not know this woman. He'd have remembered something about her if he did. There was plenty to remember, then again maybe he'd forgotten it on purpose.

"Well, you don't know me exactly, but I know you. I've been reading Molly Popp's articles. She *sayed* you were ready to find a wife. Well, here I am to put my name in the hat."

Bob felt his toes start tingling. Like a slow boil building in a pan of water, he could feel anger rolling up his body.

"I'm looking for a husband. I know this sounds weird, me showing up like this, but a girl needs to throw caution to the wind when she sees something *special.*"

He was certain he had misunderstood what the woman was saying. At least, he was hoping he'd misunderstood what the woman had said. But as she leaned toward him, smiling brightly and with what looked like not only a blinking problem, but now a supersonic twitch in her left eye, he bit back a groan. His hearing was perfectly fine and the woman was not afflicted with some bewildering twitching disorder.

She was afflicted with something, though, and it was connected straight to Molly Popp.

Fighting back anger at the bizarre turn his life had taken, he glanced at the kids crammed into the van. They were cute and all looked to be below school age. What was this woman thinking?

"Oh, don't worry about them." She waved at the kids. "They're not mine. I run a day care over in Ranger. You're our field trip." She clapped her hands together and gazed up at him as if he was the best thing since the zoo! "Kids," she hollered shrilly, "say hello to Bob."

Bob looked from the woman to the kids. What kind of woman was she to bring kids on such a far-fetched quest? At least they were clean and looked happy, waving at him from four different windows.

"Do their parents know—"

"Oh, Bob, funny! Certainly they do." She whacked him on the arm, her eyes doing a jig as she tilted her chin up at him. "Do you think I'd take those babies out without parental consent?" She chuckled and stepped close to him. He stepped back. "It's not like I came here to meet some stranger. I came to meet *you*. And everyone knows what a great guy you are. We've all been following along breathlessly, waiting to see if some lucky girl was gonna come along and capture your heart. And *well,* then Molly wrote that you were really, really wanting a wife. Pining away for one…" She sighed.

One eye was starting to blink faster than the other.

Bob wanted to run, but he wasn't feeling well enough.

She patted his arm again, and he noticed her fingernails were longer than his toes.

"It was actually one of my kid's moms who first suggested that I should just stop all that daydreaming I was doing, since I was the only single gal in the bunch of us, and like Meg Ryan in *Sleepless in Seattle* I should just do it. Go for it—you. She said, and I quote, 'Jana Diane Cravats, you need to just hop in the van and make that short, little seventy-mile trip out there and see if you and Bob connect.' Of course at first I said no. I couldn't do such a thing. But then everyone started encouragin' me. And so as you can *verify,* here I am."

She was here all right. Bob took a step back, glancing over his shoulder, estimating the paces between him and his truck. Why had he parked so far away? "I'm sorry, miss. Real sorry. But there's been a terrible mistake." Spinning, he had taken two strides toward safety when the loopy woman sprang in front of him, thrusting a pink plastic-wrapped package at him. "Here. I baked you a buttermilk pound cake. I don't want to brag, but I bake the best cakes around." She forced the cake on him, waving her hand at the purple card taped to the center. "I know this is all kooky. Especially since you're shy and all." Her eyes started up again. "But, that's my name and phone number inside the card, along with a couple of pictures of me. I wouldn't want you to confuse me with someone else." *Someone else?* Who else? Bob didn't see that happening in a million years. For Molly's sake, there better not be any others to get this one confused with!

The unmistakable roar of a motorcycle racing down his country road drowned out the rest of Jana Diane's words. She whirled around to see the motorcycle and almost fell off her shoes.

Stuck holding the pound cake, he gaped as the sparkling machine growled to a halt five feet from him. This did not look good. A woman in leather slowly removed her helmet, losing a cascade of golden hair to swing free as she slung her fringe-clad leg over the bike and stood up. Watching her stride toward him, Bob got a sick feeling. In her right hand she carried a black paper gift bag with yellow polka dots and yellow fuzzy fur lining the top. With her muscular build and the ominous look of her getup, the bag was about as out of place as it would have been if Arnold Schwarzenegger had been carrying it.

A sinking feeling in his gut, Bob again gauged the distance left between him and his truck.

"Bob baby! I'd recognize you anywhere," she boomed. And before he could make his move, she launched herself at him—*just took a flying leap straight at him!*

The buzzer on the oven sounded and not a moment too soon. Molly was starving. Poking her pencil behind her ear, she compared the notes on her yellow legal pad to the copy on her laptop, then pressed the save button, relieved to take a break. She'd forced herself to put words on paper, refusing to give in to the notion that she had writer's block. Determined to prove she could move past worrying about Bob, she'd relaxed her mind with her last-resort nonwriting activity.

Her efforts had paid off and she'd spent the past two hours hunched over the computer typing like a mad woman. But, she loved lasagna, and within seconds of the buzzer sounding, she'd slid her mitts on and lifted the spicy dish from the oven. She was about to put the store-bought garlic bread in the oven when someone started pounding on her front door. Glancing at her disaster of a kitchen, she tugged the mitts off and tossed them onto the counter, and hurried to the door. The last time someone had banged on her door like this, Lilly Wells was having her baby downstairs in Miss Adela's living quarters. Molly could still see the sheer terror on Cort Wells's face as he yelled for help. She was at least glad there couldn't be a replay of that night happening—no one she knew of was expecting a baby. Her readers had loved the article she'd written, though. As a matter of fact, she'd freelanced several fun and enlightening magazine pieces from that encounter. It had been a very profitable experience for her.

Swinging the door open now, she was shocked. Bob Jacobs was the last person she expected to see standing there. "Bob," she gasped, stepping back and reaching for the chain at her neck. The sudden thudding of her heart and the rush of heat to her face was immediate. Willing her nerves to settle back down, she studied him.

He stood with one hand stretched above his head, gripping the doorjamb, his weight leaning heavy on one hip, his other hand in midair about to come down and do more damage to her door. The distraught flash in his eyes wasn't a look she'd ever seen before.

"What's wrong?" she asked, backing up as he stormed inside and kicked the door shut with his boot.

"What's wrong? *What's wrong!*" he tore his Stetson off his head, gripping it tightly with both hands. His hair was disheveled and she noticed something red smudged on his cheek. "Do you know that I had people—*women!*—at my house. Kids. Yes kids. She had a van full of them. And cakes. There was cake."

He was so distraught that he was rambling. His navy eyes were almost black with anger—as they seemed to be a lot lately—and his eyebrows were crinkled together. Even though the man had backed her into a corner, literally, she had the overwhelming urge to smooth the stress right out of those eyebrows.

"What's wrong with you, Molly?"

"Me?" She was afraid to ask.

He halted his pacing and took a step back from her, looking shell-shocked. "You don't even know what you've done, do you?"

His question was quiet, miserable. He blinked and, to her chagrin, she was again caught off guard by how devastatingly good-looking he was. Even distraught. Distraught—the man was upset and she was noticing how handsome he was! What *was* wrong with her?

"Don't smile."

Was she smiling? How could she be smiling when he was obviously broken up about something?

"There's nothing to smile about," he growled. "Women are coming to my house bringing me cakes."

"Excuse me. Say that again please." All traces of smile were wiped away with the mention of cakes.

"*Reporters!* You heard me."

The way he said the word was far from complimentary.

"All reporters care about is getting their stories out. Who cares about the people who get messed up because of them?"

Molly covered her face with her hand, then rubbed it hard across her eyes. "The woman in the minivan," she groaned. Looking up, she met his accusing glare. "The one full of kids?"

"Yeah, you saw her?"

She choked on air and dropped her hand back to tug on the chain. "Well, I almost got run over by her. I mean she was obviously in a hurry to see you and she was zooming though town like, well, anyway...she came to your house?"

"Her and her *day care*."

"You mean those weren't all her kids?"

"Nope." He rocked back on his boot heels. "I was the field trip. Did you get that? I was the *field trip!*" He glared at her and held up a finger in salute. "*With parental consent.*"

The words were miserable sounding, and he looked angry and befuddled at the same time. And to Molly's shame and surprise she wanted to put her arms around him and comfort him. To push the lock of hair out of his eye...*okay, hold it. You are backed into a corner, he's upset with you and you are thinking about comforting him. Yeah, right. Like he would want you to. Wake up, Molly. The man has a less-than-good attitude when it comes to reporters—especially you!*

She snapped out of the daydream, straightening to her full five-eight and squaring her shoulders. "So, she brought you cake."

His expression shifted to blank disbelief. "And Motorcycle Tammy brought me lemon squares, in a fuzzy bag." He shook his head as if trying to get the picture out of his mind.

The motorcycle! Molly groaned inwardly. "Oh no! I saw her, too. They actually came to your house?" She hadn't ever thought this far in advance. Mule Hollow folks had hosted several functions and invited women to come and participate. As she had, they'd envisioned women moving here and settling. They hadn't envisioned stalkers. Or realized that giving out people's addresses might not be the smartest thing to do. But it was a small town, after all.

"Yeah, they came to my house, or at least my gate. Thankfully they didn't cross the cattle guard like someone I know."

Nope, in her wildest dreams she hadn't thought the women would come acting crazy. What had she done? So many things ran through Molly's mind. Had she put Bob in jeopardy? Strange women were coming to his house. Cassie was one thing, but Molly had overlooked the seriousness of her actions. "Bob, I promise, I never meant to cause trouble for you." She laid her palm on his forearm, feeling the sinewy muscles tense beneath her fingers. He inhaled slowly, the cotton of his red shirt stretching across his work-toned chest as he visibly reined in his turmoil.

"Look," he said at last. "I know you didn't mean

anything bad to happen. I've been driving around for the last couple of hours trying to fight off this anger but I couldn't. I even worked on my barn for a while trying not to blow up like this at you. But Molly…"

His troubled gaze dropped to her hand then returned to her face. Silence wedged between them and Molly waited for him to speak again. It was apparent that words were still forthcoming.

"Those women practically got into a fight over me. The motorcycle woman even did a little shaky kind of dance thing so I would remember how well all her fringed parts worked." His expression was glum. "And *that* was after she launched herself at me like I was an *ice-cream cone* or something. Do you know how hard I had to work to make her turn me loose? The only reason she did was because the daycare lady got jealous and distracted her. I'm telling you, Molly, they're kooks. And the worst part of it is the crazy daycare lady had encouragement from all the mothers of the kids she keeps! Can you believe that?"

Molly dropped her hand from his arm and waved weakly toward the kitchen. She knew he was searching for the right words, trying not to let his temper get the best of him. One of Bob Jacobs's strong points—and he had many—was his normally calm, almost innocent charm. Not really shy, more like he usually thought things out before saying something he would regret. She had somehow found the buttons that pushed him to his limit. And for that she was sorry. Thinking how hard he'd tried not to come here and vent at her she felt she owed him something.

"I baked lasagna," she blurted out, wanting to calm him, to ease the anger he was fighting to control. "I know it feeds an army and you know how it is when you live alone..." She'd said she was sorry—maybe he would accept a token of that remorse. "Would...would you like to join me?"

Why was she inviting him for dinner? He was going to turn her down flat. No way would he say yes to the woman who had single-handedly turned his perfect life upside down. She deserved the startled look he gave her. But he deserved so much more than the way she'd treated him that she pushed forward. More certain than before that she wanted him to stay.

"Really, please stay. Honestly, I'm not great in the kitchen, but I've been told I make decent lasagna. Dinner is the least I can do to say I'm sorry for causing you all this trouble."

And she really was sorry.

He thumped his hat on his hip, studying her for a minute...no doubt wondering what had possessed her to think he would ever consider such an offer from her.

Molly bit her lip and prepared for rejection.

"Okay."

She blinked. Twice. Molly fought off the fluttery feeling rolling over her and rubbed her hands on the front of her blue jeans to steady herself. "Good. Very good. Here, let me take your hat." She was breathless as she reached for his hat. Their fingers met and she froze for a moment. "I'll...just hang it over here and you can get it on your way out." She fumbled the hat, tearing it from his fingers. Smiling weakly, he met her gaze, and for the briefest second she thought she saw something in his eyes...then he let go and turned toward the window.

"Great view."

"I enjoy it." She couldn't move—she had imagined the spark of interest. Sure there had once been interest between them, but they were the proverbial two ships going separate directions. She'd put a lid on that attraction not long after moving here. She hadn't wanted anything standing in the way when the time came for her to move on. She'd made it clear to him that her career took priority in her life. It was the only fair thing to do. Once she'd put her priorities out there, it had been like a breaker blowout for him. The man had visibly shut down all interest on a personal level. It had been instant and firm.

It hadn't stopped her curiosity though, and when someone mentioned once that his dad had been a reporter, she'd been shocked to realize his dad was Ted Jacobs. He'd been a freelancer whose work had appeared in prestigious magazines and newspapers for nearly thirty years. Molly had long admired his work—the man had had a knack for penetrating high-voltage situations. He'd lived on the edge of danger throughout his nearly thirty-year career, writing stories that touched lives and taught lessons in humanity at the same time. Molly completely respected him.

Studying Bob's back, she wondered what life had been like growing up with a famous father like that. It was none of her business, so she tried to cap her curiosity as she placed his hat on the small table beside the door and focused on feeding him. Taking a deep breath, she moved to the kitchen and placed the garlic bread into the oven to warm.

Grateful that he'd moved the topic onto something less volatile between them, she went with it. "Since I was the first renter in the building, I was able to choose the best view. It's nice to look out there and see past the town's roofline to the horizon. The sunsets are spectacular."

"I bet," he said, coming to the doorway. "Can I help—whoa. What happened here?"

HOLD ME, COWBOY

Molly glanced at the sink full of bowls and the counter covered in flour. Of all days for him to come to her apartment. She sighed.

"I take cooking classes sometimes."

His eyebrows knit together again, in curiosity this time. "Where?"

Molly bit her lip and rocked back on her heels. "On TV. I pick one of the shows on a cooking channel and I try something. On days I'm thinking out article kinks, I bake bread. It relaxes me."

"Ahh, so that explains the counters and this."

He reached out and brushed her cheek with his thumb. Molly hiccupped and immediately swung toward the faucet to get a glass of water to hide the surprise on her face. She hadn't had hiccups in years, but that wasn't what had surprised her.

"So you made the bread. Cool."

She finished gulping the water and holding her breath at the same time. "No. It's store-bought bread." When she turned around, breathing normal again, his gaze was roaming the room. "So did you eat all the homemade bread?"

Why couldn't he have come over *after* she'd cleaned up her mess? Sure, he was looking for Suzy Homemaker and she wasn't her—and she didn't care to be her—but did he have to find out that even if she'd wanted to be, she still wouldn't be anywhere close to being Suzy?

What did it matter? "I can't bake bread. I try. I make huge messes and I try at least once a month, whether I'm having trouble with an article or not. But I can't bake bread. The bread doesn't take it personally since I can't cook much else, either." There, the cat was out of the bag. Why she cared that she was no good at something she had no desire to be good at confused her, and always had.

"I didn't take you as the kind of woman who wanted to be in the kitchen." He had that baffled sound in his voice.

"Well, actually, that's a gray area with me. I don't have a clue if I do or don't."

He chuckled, and it sounded wonderful to Molly's ears. Bob always had been one to laugh easily and lately she'd taken that away. Standing beside him in her tiny kitchen, her ears warmed suddenly and her stomach rolled again.

"Um, do you still want to help?" she asked, needing to change the subject.

"Sure."

"Then grab the place mats out of that drawer there—" she pointed behind him "—and the flatware there." She pointed to the drawer above the other one.

HOLD ME, COWBOY

"I'll get the glasses. Is iced tea okay with you?"

"That's my drink of choice."

"Sweet or unsweet?"

"The sweeter the better. But I'll drink it either way."

"You're in luck. I learned to make tea from my mom and it's as sweet as it can get without being syrup."

Within minutes she was taking the bread out of the oven and setting it on the table beside the lasagna.

She shouldn't have been surprised when Bob pulled her chair out for her, then waited until she was settled before seating himself.

Watching him, Molly only realized she'd twisted the chain at her neck to the point of breaking when it pinched her skin. It had been a long time since she'd shared dinner with a man and she knew it was pathetically apparent.

"May I say the blessing?" he asked softly.

"Please."

He reached across the table his palm upturned. Molly stared at it before placing hers in it. She immediately bowed her head to hide the panic in her eyes. This was so cozy. So Norman Rockwell perfect. She listened as Bob asked God's blessing over the food.

It was a simple prayer but it was a prayer from a man comfortable with his Lord. It should have relaxed her— it didn't. When he released her hand, she snatched it back so fast she knocked her tea over.

"Oh," she gasped. Springing up, she hit her knees on the table and if he hadn't had quick hands his tea would have toppled too.

"I'm so sorry." She snagged a dish towel off the counter and started mopping up the mess. She was not normally a klutz, well, not exactly. Fortunately it was one of her smaller glasses and she had it cleaned up before it spread to his side of the table. He was nice enough not to kid her about the accident and within moments she was back in her seat.

Sweating.

"Okay," she said, her heart still pounding from humiliation. Children spilled their drinks. "Let's try this again. I'm not normally so clumsy."

He grinned, showing his dimples. "It's okay. Really."

She took a deep breath, clasped her hands together in her lap and willed herself to relax. What was wrong with her? She must be coming down with something. Fever, trembling hands. Her stomach was all weird feeling and she was thinking fuzzy. She just hoped she didn't make Bob sick. Poor man, she'd done enough to him already without giving him the flu.

Or whatever in the world was wrong with her.

CHAPTER SEVEN

Molly was acting strange. Bob wondered if she was coming down with something. She didn't look sick though. She looked like she always looked to him—beautiful. Maybe a little flushed. But that only enhanced her beauty. With skin the color of a golden apricot, her rust-colored hair and those green eyes it was no wonder every cowboy around couldn't take his eyes off her when she entered a room. But they kept their distance, just like him. Molly was merely passing through and all the guys could tell she wasn't staying. It showed in her eyes, in the distance lurking there.

But right now she was acting odd. Maybe he'd hurt her feelings about her cooking. He'd probably looked pretty astounded by her revelation that she was even attempting anything in the kitchen. *Of course* he had been astounded. Amazed. A little bewildered, to be honest.

And the fact she had an ongoing battle with trying to make bread...now that was cute. Not that any of it mattered. She was leaving. He needed to keep remembering that—and the not-so-tiny matter that she might have done irreparable damage to his anonymity. Not that he wanted total obscurity, but he didn't want to become the Mule Hollow field trip, either.

"This is good," he said, taking a bite of the steaming pasta. "You weren't kidding."

She paused with her fork midair. "That's the only thing I can boast about. Believe me."

He laughed and watched her take a small bite. "I doubt that. Maybe you can't bake bread, but most people can't. I guess I should have brought dessert, especially since I happen to have plenty of it now." Now why'd he go and do that? He'd just said the prayer and he was actually relaxing.

Molly tensed immediately at the reference to his zealous visitors.

"I am sorry." Setting her fork on her plate, she picked up her napkin and dabbed at her mouth. Worry filled her eyes.

"I'll live. Relax, and forget I said anything...although, daycare lady did say she was a great baker. A guy couldn't go wrong marrying a great baker. Just look at Brady—the man has the best of both worlds since Dottie is a baker *and* a candy maker. Maybe I could get lucky." He smiled—the day did have its comical points.

Molly's shoulders relaxed and she put the napkin back down, smoothing out the wrinkles she'd wrung into it. "Yeah. You have a point there. Um, I've been meaning to tell you that there's something red on your cheek."

Bob lifted his napkin and rubbed his left cheek. She shook her head and pointed to her own opposite cheek. He rubbed his other cheek and stared at the red lipstick on the white napkin. "Aw, man! I've had that on here the whole time?"

She nodded, her eyes dancing. "Those bakers are dangerous women."

"You don't know the half of it." He wanted to forget the crazy women. "Truth is, I don't know from which of the women I got kissed. When the daycare lady got jealous of the motorcycle lady, she literally tried to wedge herself between the two of us like a human crowbar...all I was concentrating on was getting away from both of them."

Molly's eyes grew serious. "I am sincerely sorry. But they know a good thing when they see it." She smiled then frowned as if she'd realized what she'd said. Suddenly she seemed uneasy again.

Feeling the same, Bob searched for something else to talk about, realizing he wanted to talk about Molly. Despite everything, she intrigued him. He surveyed the apartment she called home. *Home* wasn't quite the word he would use to describe the rooms. A furnished place would come with more than she had here. The lack of belongings baffled him.

Her walls were bare. There was nothing on the side tables. There *was* a bookshelf full of books, but other than that there was nothing in the room that said someone actually lived in the apartment. The only adornment on the coffee table was her laptop and an open folder with a yellow legal pad on top of it.

"You haven't unpacked yet, or are you moving?" He took a bite of garlic bread. Maybe she was already leaving and he hadn't heard the news yet.

She glanced around and smiled. "It's bad, isn't it? No, on both counts. I keep saying I'm going to go out and buy a bunch of those accessories that the home-improvement channels are always going on about. Maybe a plant. But I'm not much of a homey person and I'd probably kill it."

"You mean, this is how you plan to keep the room?" She looked blank.

"Well, I'm not much of a shopper, either. It takes

time to buy all that stuff. And well—"

She shrugged.

Bob laughed. She was so serious. "Don't you want to make your house comfortable?" She called creature comforts *stuff* as if it was a dirty word.

He didn't mean to make her feel bad, but when she put her fork down, placed her hands in her lap and scanned the room, he suddenly wished he could take back his question. What was up with him and his big mouth? When she met his gaze, he knew he'd hurt her feelings and she was struggling not to let it show.

"I'm a buffoon. What you do in your home is your business. One man's comfort is another man's burden. Right?" He smiled, hoping to chase away the past five minutes.

"I guess so." Her brows were crinkled toward each other as she scanned her lack of things. "I write. That's what I do. I write. I research and I write some more. I guess my priorities are different than some."

"You don't want roots?" *Hey, Jacobs, back off. You know the answer to that. You've been here, remember.*

"As I told you when I first came here, I want to travel."

"That's right, Mule Hollow is just a stepping stone for you." *There you go, Jacobs, keep kicking up trouble.*

She dropped her head slightly. "Well, um, I recognize Mule Hollow as a huge resource. I look on it as a gift. Not just because God's given me the opportunity to help the town and at the same time help promote my writing, but because this is where I met Jesus."

The sincerity in her voice and her expression had him pushing more. "But you still don't think Mule Hollow is the place to settle down in—here, among friends?"

She picked up her fork and pushed her food around in her plate. "Look. I used to hide in my closet…and dream. I mean, I would picture places in my mind that I would travel to when I grew up and could get away. Places where I could make a difference. I want to tell stories that help link the world together like a community. You know, build a bond, help make a bridge between all people…"

And that was well and good, but it still meant never landing in one spot. "You do have a knack for writing a story people want to get involved in. Believe me, I've found that out firsthand."

She blushed again, a very becoming shade of pink. "And for that I am so sorry. Again."

How could he stay mad at her? He never was one

to hold a grudge. Except maybe with his father. When a man chose career over family it was pretty cut-and-dried. Truth was, at times he still struggled with that grudge. He knew it wasn't right, but it was the truth.

"What about marriage. You still don't have plans to ever marry?"

She took the last bite of her food and shook her head one hard jerk. "Not me. I'm committed. And I do feel called to write. Until I realized I'd been basically living my life on my terms and not the Lord's, I was just focused on my career and what it could do for me. I didn't have the entire picture. After I accepted the Lord, I was praying for guidance and suddenly everything became clear to me. What I write can do all that I'd hoped for—with a twist. I do it for Him now. I want my stories to show God's power."

She paused and took a deep breath. "That's why I got so excited about what you're doing. Your faith shows that power. Your words were inspiring. You represent all of those who want to find love, but you want it to be with the woman that God chooses for you. You are on a quest much higher than merely finding a companion. And you're willing to sacrifice to find her. If everyone did that, maybe things would be different."

She had a way about her.

"I don't call it sacrifice. It's not sacrifice when

you're working toward getting something you really want. And I want a family. It's all I've ever wanted."

"And I know you didn't like my stories about you, but that was all I was trying to help you get. I know, I know, you don't need my help. But don't you think that my being here could have been to specifically help you? I mean, God could use my storyline to bring you the woman of your dreams."

She was tenacious. "Maybe," he responded. "But I never figured my future wife would wear fringed leather." He couldn't deny grinning.

Molly smiled and winked at him. "You never know what God has in store for you, Bob."

He looked at her with total assurance. "I can tell you it's not anything I saw today. And that's for sure."

"Well, there's always tomorrow."

The sun was just going down when Bob walked up the brick path to his back porch. Scooping John Boy up out of a makeshift pen beside the steps, he ruffled the silky hair then opened the door and strode into his house.

"Hey, little fella, did you miss me?" He liked the idea of coming home to something other than his horses and his cows. A dog wasn't a family, but it was the beginnings of a unit.

He stopped in the kitchen and surveyed the open space. He'd only been living here for a month, but unlike Molly's apartment, it looked as if he'd lived here all his life. He'd hung pictures on the walls, even put flowers in the entrance hall. The lady at the store in Ranger where he'd shopped for many items had first told him the particular vase of silk flowers were only for display.

However, after he'd spent a couple of months' pay in the store she'd given him the large vase of flowers as a thank-you. They now looked very welcoming in the center of the small table in his foyer.

He liked the way it looked. The flowers reminded him of springtime and cheer. And that was exactly the kind of feeling he wanted when he walked into his home.

He and Molly looked at life like polar opposites. He knew exactly why he wanted his house to feel like a home. His past was directly responsible for wanting to feel comforted by his surroundings. He wanted the security of a home with roots set deep in the Texas soil. He wanted to bring a family up here in this solid small community and know that his kids would always understand they had a place to come home to. He'd chosen Mule Hollow carefully as he'd toured the country as a rodeo bullfighter. It had been a weird feeling when he'd stepped out of his beat-up truck six years ago and felt connected.

The poor town. The memory of how sad it had looked then amazed him. It had been pitiful with its worn-down buildings and deserted streets, but it had called to something deep in his soul, something inside of himself that related.

He hadn't quit the circuit that day, had continued on to his finals in Las Vegas. But he'd known he'd found what he'd been searching for and he'd quit the PBR at the end of the week, returning to Mule Hollow immediately. Clint Matlock had hired him on and taught him everything he knew about ranching. And it was enough to make him feel confident enough to make a go of it with his own place.

He'd been planning his life ever since the day his dad left him at boarding school. His mother had died and his dad had chosen his career over his kid. That left Bob with no options but to play the game the way it was dealt. He'd been stuck in a room with another kid, had meals in a cafeteria every day, spent most holidays either at the school or at a roommate's family gathering, and on occasion shared a dinner with his dad. That is, when his dad could find time between world-class assignments to fit in his son.

HOLD ME, COWBOY

Bob had been angry about that part of his life for years. Rebellion had driven him to bull riding. Some guys rode for the joy of the ride, or the adrenaline. He'd ridden as an outlet for rage. It had taken God's love to redeem him from the pit of anger. But, just because he wasn't bearing the fury of a loveless childhood anymore didn't mean he wasn't still angry looking back. He had his moments. And he didn't have patience for parents who didn't give their kids the love and attention they deserved. His kids were going to get more love than they would know what to do with.

At least he had to admire Molly—she hadn't said she wanted a family. He might not understand her choice of work over family, but he could respect that she knew she couldn't have both. Not in the world she was seeking as a career.

Looking around his cozy home, a sense of satisfaction eased over him. He'd come out on this end of his life with a solid understanding of what he did and didn't want. And one thing was certain. He wanted a traditional wife to fill his traditional home with love and children.

He held John Boy up in the air and smiled at him. His bright golden eyes and lopsided grin cheered him. Border collies were the best dogs a man could have. They were excellent cattle dogs and great with children. Bob's hope was by the time John Boy was a year old Bob would have found the love of his life.

"She's out there, John Boy. Yes she is."

The puppy turned his head to the side and his lips drooped into a frown as he studied Bob innocently.

"Oh, you don't believe me." Bob tilted his forehead to meet the pup's and rubbed soothingly. "I'm telling you she's out there. And believe me I'm more than ready to make her acquaintance."

Molly was sitting at a picnic table outside Sam's. Her computer sat open in front of her. She was happily finishing up a feature article for *Countryside Magazine*. She'd had to keep focusing her thoughts, but she'd finally come up with a great article. It wasn't *Time Magazine,* but it was a good article and it would pay the bills.

Sitting in the warm sunshine, with a soft drink beside her and one deadline met, her thoughts drifted to where they'd tried time and again to go all morning. To Bob.

It had been two days since she'd seen him and she'd thought of their dinner together often. It had been such a surprising evening, and bits and pieces of it had snuck into her thoughts ever since, distracting her from her work. Like Bob taking her hand to say grace. She'd analyzed it from different angles, finally realizing the reason she'd been so nervous that evening was simply due to the fact that Bob really was a man seeking God and working his faith. It wasn't just a show.

And she couldn't deny the fact that she found that very attractive in a man.

She'd never had a man in her life who was the initiator of faith. The simple act of offering to give thanks to the Lord for his meal had touched her heart. Molly's own father had been the instigator of wrath and trembling in her home. Though he'd never been physically violent, he'd enjoyed turmoil. When he was unhappy he wanted her mother to be unhappy.

And Molly, well, she was an afterthought. She couldn't remember one memory of him spending time with her. Her mother had explained away his lack of interest with the excuse that Nelson Popp hadn't wanted children, but since her mother *had* wanted a child, he'd given her one. So Molly was her mother's special gift. Funny how she'd never felt very special. One of the many things about Mule Hollow that had drawn her was the fact that the cowboys wanted wives and families. When she'd arrived that first day she'd recognized a group of people excited and committed to not only building up a community, but more important, a community committed to building up families. She'd been hooked—from a writer's viewpoint, that is.

Watching the genuine love between all the couples who'd married since she'd moved to town had given her a new version of what life centered around Christ could be like. But until Bob had asked her to pray with him sitting at her own table, she'd not experienced or even thought about it for herself.

And she wasn't thinking about it now, she insisted. She had dreams, goals, things she had to accomplish. Places she wanted to see and experience. Lives she wanted to touch with the words she put to paper. God had a plan for her life and she couldn't allow herself to get distracted. Not even by Bob.

"Molly! Yoo-hoo, Molly." Esther Mae Wilcox, her red hair flaring out from the sides, came hustling down the walk toward her. Recently Lacy had given Esther a new style that *had* been gorgeous. Sadly though, most days it looked as if it'd been sent through the fluff cycle in the clothes dryer—with Esther Mae attached.

Today was no different. It fanned out on both sides in uneven wings, making her look as if she was moments away from taking flight.

"What's up, Esther Mae?"

"I never did get to talk to you about getting attacked by Bob's bull."

Molly closed the computer screen. "I'm fine, Esther Mae. Don't worry about me."

Esther Mae sat down at the green picnic table and faced Molly.

"Bob rescued you." Esther paused dramatically, her hair-wings fluttering at the sides. "Jumped right out in the center of that raging bull's path and rescued you. Whip cracking. It's straight out of the movies romantic. Don't you think it's *Indiana Jones* romantic?"

So she wasn't the only one who put Bob and Indy in the same category. The word *romantic,* however, brought Molly away from daydreaming like a shot with a crooked needle. "Not romantic, Esther Mae. Heroic, yes." Indiana Jones heroic!

"It's the same thing. Why, the way Bob charged in there and rescued you from that bloodthirsty bull just makes my heart go thumpety-thump, thump."

"Now, hold on, Esther Mae. Don't get carried away. Remember, it was his bull in the first place. What was he supposed to do, let me get creamed right there in front of his house? There's nothing romantic about self-preservation."

Esther Mae harrumphed. "Now come on, Molly. You know you like the man. Why, you write the most dazzling things about him all the time. A person can't write that way and not like someone in a special way."

"Dazzling. Where did that come from? I write the facts. And the fact is that Bob is a nice guy who will make some woman a really great husband one day."

"You. How about you?"

"Me." Molly tried to play it cool—after all she'd felt this coming. Being cool was the best way. "Now Esther Mae, you need to go back over there to Heavenly Inspirations and tell Norma Sue and Lacy and Sheri… and Adela and whomever else is watching through the front glass that they can put their matchmaking caps back in the washing machine. Because if they think I'm going to be joining in the fray to make Bob mine, then obviously there's something in their hats that needs a good cleaning out."

Esther Mae frowned. "Well, I'll be. If I hadn't read the articles myself I would say some other woman wrote them." She paused, her lips dropping into a deeper frown. The line of freckles across her cheeks seemed to mimic her frown, making her disappointment doubly pronounced.

Molly watched nervously, her fears heightening as Esther's lips slowly started shifting upward and turned quickly into the smile of a crazed person. "You know he's been having visitors. Lady visitors. Bearing food." She'd been on deadline for the *Countryside* article and also her weekly column, so she hadn't allowed herself out of her apartment until this morning. It was no surprise that everyone knew about the daycare lady and Motorcycle Tammy. "Yes, I knew about the two of them. And I feel terrible—"

"Two. Honey, where have you been? Maybe two a day."

"What?" A sense of dread snared Molly. She ran a hand down her face and groaned. Two a day. Poor Bob, he must be furious. It was going to take more than a meal of her sorry cooking to fix this. Why hadn't he complained to her again? As upset as he'd been about daycare and motorcycle lady, why had he not come barging back to her apartment to vent at her again?

"I have to go, Esther Mae. See you later." She fumbled with stuffing her computer into her backpack, knowing she was being watched like a hawk by Esther Mae, who would report her weird behavior to her cohorts. But this was no time to worry about what anyone thought of her. This was about Bob and the trouble she'd brought into his life.

All she could think of was finding him and apologizing. She was halfway across the road when Esther Mae called after her through her chuckles.

"If you think the visitors are something, you should see his mail delivery!"

CHAPTER EIGHT

Letting out a long whistle, Clint stared at Bob's dining-room table. Bob was staring, too, as he'd been doing off and on for the past four hours, ever since the mail had arrived. It just wasn't right.

When he'd confessed he was ready for the Lord to send him a wife, he'd never envisioned his eight-foot-long dining-room table piled high with envelopes! There were purple envelopes, pink envelopes, envelopes with little sparkly doodads all over them, envelopes with squiggles and envelopes with flowers. And he could see a few mixed in there with kisses all over them—real or fake, he didn't plan to get close enough to find out.

And that was just what he could see from a distance. Sad but true. The sight of all that fluff and flounce was enough to make a man queasy. And if looking at the rainbow mountain of unabashed calls for attention didn't choke a cowboy down, the *smell* was enough to get the job done and then some. Bob figured all the flowery aromas emanating from the stack could knock a cowboy out of the saddle from a good twenty yards away.

And here he and Clint were standing in the same house with it!

"Oh boy, Hoss, you weren't kidding," Clint said, fanning the air with his hat. "Have you read any of them?" Getting brave, he ventured forward and, with two fingers, plucked up a green one by the corner. It was embellished with a strand of yellow flowers running across the top. Slowly he lifted it up to the light, back to his nose and sniffed. "Whoa!"

Bob watched his friend's eyes tear up.

"You're braver than me," he said, taking two steps back when Clint waved it toward him. "No way! If I'd known the mailman was hauling that across my cattle guard, I'd have made certain Sylvester was out front to run him off."

It was true. He'd been stupefied when he opened his front door to a frowning mailman who had informed him he wasn't a city mail carrier, he was rural carrier, and that meant he didn't care to make house calls but they didn't have room for the letters down at the office.

And then the skinny man had dropped the backbreaking bag at his feet. Reeling, Bob had watched him stalk to his vehicle and drive away.

Suffering from shock and unable to think of anything else to say or do, Bob had picked up the heavy tote and carried it to his table.

Clint snapped the envelope at him, bringing his wandering mind back to the present. "Come on, Bob you gotta read at least a few. Who knows? Your one true love might be waiting in that pile. Could be this pea-green one right here."

Bob didn't smile. "Knock yourself out. Go for it. My thoughts are that they're all kooks."

Clint's grin exploded and he started ripping. The sound of an approaching truck—and John Boy's yaps—gave Bob the excuse to leave Clint to read alone. As he walked to the back door to see who else had arrived for the party, Clint's chuckles followed him.

"Give me patience, Lord, and don't let this be another surprise." Or a truckload of cowhands come to gloat.

"Hey, Brady," he called, seeing his friend. The tall lawman walked up the pebbled path, looking as disgruntled as Bob felt.

"You'd better not be bringing me any more bad news," he called, stepping out onto the porch for some much-needed fresh air. John Boy scurried to him and immediately sat on his boot and leaned against his leg, growling at Brady. Bob bent down to run a reassuring hand along the puppy's back. "If you *are* bringing bad news, I'll give you five seconds to turn around and head on back to town before I set my dog on you." He grinned up at Brady before straightening and offering him his hand in greeting.

Brady shook his hand but didn't smile. "I hate to say it's not the best of news. I thought I'd give your place another drive-by before heading home. I'm sorry to tell you, but Motorcycle Tammy is out there sitting at your cattle guard again. This is spooky, Bob. That's four days she's been hanging around here. She'd set up a tent out there if I didn't run her off. My official advice is if she doesn't heed my warning and disappear, then you ought to obtain a restraining order. These days this isn't something to fool around with."

Bob braced a hand on the porch post and studied the setting sun, trying to tamp down the turmoil inside his chest. He hated to feel anger at Molly building again, but it was there. Sure, she hadn't meant any of this to happen, but it had. And he was the one paying for her lack of responsible reporting.

"I'm not scared of a woman," he said. "Tammy is one short of a full deck, but I won't believe she's dangerous. Not yet anyway."

"Don't be so sure. It's not about what you believe and don't believe. We're talking facts here, and in my days on the force in Houston I've seen tragedy happen under circumstances far less suspect."

Bob realized he might be in denial but he refused to give in to this. "We'll take it a step at a time. How's that?"

"It's your call."

Chuckles from inside the house penetrated the evening air. Bob cocked his head and slanted a glance at Brady. "That's Clint. He's reading my mail."

"Oh yeah, I heard about that. Seems you're more popular than Santa Claus. Norma Sue saw Jarvis at the diner and he pointed it out to her and the others before coming your way with it. You know what that means."

"Yeah, I know. I can hear the laughter already." Bob hung his head, realizing everyone knew what was on his table. "You go take a look and tell me if it's funny. But hold your nose."

Reluctantly he trailed behind Brady, who strode inside, as anxious as Bob was certain all of Mule Hollow was, to see the dog-and-pony show his life had turned into. Thanks to the one and only *Miss Molly Popp*.

"I didn't mean this to happen," Molly said, looking

around the salon full of women. Heavenly Inspirations was packed. Literally. Norma Sue and Esther Mae were in the styling chairs. Sheri and Adela were at the manicure table while Sheri gave Adela her weekly manicure. Lacy was leaning against the wall listening to Molly with the intensity of a master chess player. And Molly was sitting uncomfortably in the shampoo chair wishing she could crawl down the drain and drown herself. Bob had refused her calls and, though she'd been watching for him, he hadn't come to town so she had no way of apologizing. It was abundantly clear that he held her responsible.

"This isn't your fault, Molly," Norma Sue said, but her trademark smile, the one that seemed to stretch from the top of Texas to the bottom, was missing.

"Norma Sue, you know it is. If I hadn't written that article, Bob wouldn't be holed up at his ranch like a prisoner. I never thought I would say this, but thank goodness Sylvester is there to deter trespassers. Applegate and Stanley have even started calling them Bob-hunters! How horrible is that?"

It was true. The day after she and Bob had dined together at her apartment the women began showing up, one or two a day, and some hadn't gone away. Specifically Motorcycle Tammy. Why, at this very moment she was down the street at Sam's, eating. And it was killing Applegate and Stanley, since they weren't inside getting the scoop. Because of their mysterious on-going feud with Sam, the two old-timers had left their checkers on the picnic table in front of Pete's and could be seen hovering at the window of the diner, watching from outside. They refused to go inside even though it was obvious their curiosity was eating them alive. It was pathetic.

"Molly, don't fret," Esther Mae said, breaking into her morose thoughts. Molly glanced at her in time to see her patting her hair. Though Lacy had long since cut off Esther Mae's beehive that had jiggled and swayed with her every movement, the habit of patting it to make sure it was still hitched tight to her head was ingrained in Esther's DNA. "Bob said he wanted a wife. The boy is just going to have to get used to the idea that there is obviously an overwhelming bunch of females who would love the position. It's like that movie with Tom Hanks where the son calls into the radio station trying to get his dad a new wife. Oh, I just loved that movie. Saw it again just last night. Of course it would be nice if some of these gals were normal. You think in your next article you could specifically state those without a brain need not apply."

"It's not that they don't have brains, Esther Mae," Norma Sue snapped. "It's simply that God gave ants much more common sense than He chose to give these poor gals."

Esther Mae looked at Norma Sue as if she'd come from another planet. "Norma Sue. *Normal women* don't tape signs on the sides of their cars with the slogan Marry Me, Bob. And what about yesterday when that woman had that trunk full of speakers and she plum started a stampede out at his ranch while she played love songs to the poor guy. That ain't a lack of common sense. That's dingier than a dingbat right there." Norma Sue shook her head.

"So says you. It might take spunky personalities like that to round out Bob's calm, quiet personality."

Molly figured she'd demolished that sweet part of Bob's personality.

"Ladies," Adela said in her soft voice of reason. "Getting yourselves in a dither isn't going to solve anything."

Molly listened to the two friends debate and she had to agree with Esther Mae on this one, which was unusual. She would have believed that Norma Sue would think the women were crazy and that Esther Mae would have found their behavior normal. The fact that the debate was completely upside down was just par for the course of this entire trip into loopyland. But, either way, normal women didn't do the crazy things Bob's suitors had done. They didn't take a vanload of preschoolers on a field trip to see a bachelor. After all, Bob wasn't a puppy in a window or a monkey in a cage. Although, because of her, he was probably feeling like one.

Esther Mae frowned. "Adela, I'm not in a dither. And to be fair to Norma, I have to agree that the woman in the wedding dress might need a little professional guidance."

"Esther Mae, hush," Norma Sue snapped, glancing at Molly.

The knot in the pit of Molly's stomach tightened. "What woman in a wedding dress?" She hadn't heard about this one. She scanned the room, which had suddenly gone quite as a courtroom hearing a verdict. Sheri was suddenly concentrating a little too hard on the manicure she was giving Adela and even Adela looked as if she was in prayer. Which meant she was seeking guidance from the Lord or praying for intervention. Molly's inquiring eyes settled on Lacy.

The blonde dynamo suddenly looked like she'd swallowed bad milk. "Now, Molly, don't get worked up over this."

Those words confirmed Molly's suspicion that something more had happened, something she wasn't going to like. The fact that Lacy's pink fingernails were tapping double time on her hipbone proved it further. Lacy ran a hand through her hair, glanced around the room then met Molly's gaze. "Okay, I'll tell you, but please don't freak out. Everything is fine. It really is. God is in control of everything that's happening. Yes, it might be a little weird. Yes, it might not be the straightest path to finding the right woman for Bob, but the Lord is still in control."

Molly stood up. "Lacy, tell me what has happened that I don't know about. Please."

"Applegate and Stanley saw a woman wearing a wedding dress come into town yesterday afternoon. You know how they are suffering because they aren't in the big thick of things down at Sam's. So as we've all seen, even though they aren't down at the diner, they can see plenty from the picnic table in front of the feed store. They can at least watch who comes and goes at the diner. And well, Sam confirmed what they've been telling everyone—that a woman wearing a satin wedding dress and a tiara came into the diner yesterday."

How had she missed this?

There was a collective sigh that skipped around the room. If this was true then Molly had single-handedly turned Bob Jacobs's life into a fiasco.

And this was on top of the already scary reality that

Bob may literally have a stalker on his hands. Sheriff Brady had had to make several trips to Bob's to tell Motorcycle Tammy she couldn't stake a claim on Bob's property. Or Bob. The woman had tried three nights in a row to actually pitch a tent in the ditch beside Bob's cattle guard!

She scared Molly. She was too intense...a normal woman didn't throw herself at a man the first time she saw him. And Bob had said he'd had to do more fancy footwork to avoid being captured by her than he'd done in any arena at a bullfighting competition. That was scary.

Then there were the cakes. The mailman was in a tizzy. He'd delivered more perishables to Bob's in a week than he'd delivered in his entire twenty years on the job. Not to mention the hefty bags of cards and letters still coming. Esther Mae was right in some comparisons to the movie *Sleepless in Seattle*. Both Tom Hanks and Bob had received loads of mail, but this wasn't a movie. This was real life—*Bob's* life—and Molly may have put it in jeopardy.

It didn't matter that she hadn't meant to, that her intentions had been honorable. In the movie, the response had been a flood of marriage proposals by sympathetic women, and Tom's character had eventually found the perfect woman. But again, this was no movie. This was real life, and if Bob's Miss Right *did* happen to respond to anything she'd written in her articles, it wouldn't matter. She would be lost in the circus that Molly had created!

It was all too stupid to be real, but sadly, being stupid didn't make it go away. It was very much reality and she had to find a way to make it right. She had to. "Molly, come with me." Lacy grabbed her by the hand and pulled her from her chair. "I think you need destressing. And that means a ride in my pink Cadillac."

Molly thought about resisting. But Lacy loved to ride in her pink 1958 Cadillac convertible. And though Molly was touched by her efforts to cheer her, she hated to tell Lacy that even a ride in her precious car couldn't fix the mess she'd created. But she couldn't find an excuse not to go, especially with Lacy dragging her and everyone else practically pushing her out the door to where the Caddy sat like a big pink life raft.

Lacy sprang over the driver's door in her trademark *Dukes of Hazard* style and grinned at Molly like a schoolgirl from behind the steering wheel.

"Come on, Molly, time's a wastin'."

"Hop in there and stop worrying," Norma Sue said, giving her a little nudge.

Molly sat on the edge of the door, lifted her legs over

and plopped down onto the white leather of the passenger seat. Everyone, knowing the way Lacy drove, stepped away from the vehicle and waved.

"I don't know why I'm doing this," she groaned as Lacy cranked the motor and revved the engine. She didn't comment, just stomped on the gas pedal and shot them backward out of the parking space like a bottle rocket on the Fourth of July.

"Molly, I feel the need for speed, so sit back, buckle up and let your mind ease while you talk to the Lord about how you're feeling. Then we'll talk."

They had only gone about a half a mile from town when Motorcycle Tammy pulled up beside them.

She had on black leather pants and a coat with fringe waving in the wind. The fringe she'd made dance for Bob. "What's she doing?" Molly gasped, watching in surprise as she saluted them then gunned the shiny purple bike and exploded past them at a speed Molly could only describe as insane.

"Do you think she's going to Bob's?" Lacy called over the wind and the roar of the disappearing motorcycle.

"If I were a betting woman I'd say yes. Does she not know her welcome is worn-out?"

"Doesn't look like she cares." Lacy glanced over at her with an expression that asked what Molly wanted to do about it.

"This isn't right, Lacy. Just because I wrote an article doesn't give her the right to badger poor Bob like this."

"No, it doesn't. None of us meant for this kind of harassment to happen when we started the 'wives wanted' campaign."

"Then that does it, Lacy! Follow that motorcycle." Molly sat up in her seat, keeping the bike in her sights as it steadily pulled away from them in the distance. "I've had it, Lacy. I did this to Bob and I'm going to fix it. First thing in the morning I'll write a full-fledged apology to him in my column, and in a nice but firm way let everyone know that while Mule Hollow has many eligible bachelors, there is a certain protocol that needs to be followed. But first, we need to catch up with Speedy and tell her to back off. This has gone on long enough!"

Needing no further encouragement Lacy grinned at her. "Hold on to your shoestrings 'cause here we go." When Lacy stomped on the gas, the power of the old Caddy knocked Molly back in the seat like a bug on a windshield. Lacy was laughing and, despite the speed with which the scenery was flying by, Molly couldn't help smiling.

And then she saw Motorcycle Tammy whip her bike onto the drive up to Bob's house and continue on over the cattle guard.

"What is she doing?" Molly gasped, all laughter gone.

"Looks like trouble to me. Do you see Sylvester anywhere?"

Molly scanned the pasture as Lacy eased off the gas. "Nope. Thank goodness. Come on, we have to go after her."

"You got it, sister. This is more adventure than I've had since I went after the cattle rustlers!"

Molly almost bit her tongue as they careened over the irksome cattle guard. The memory of her last encounter on this side of the fence had her looking in both directions to make certain Sylvester didn't materialize out of thin air as he'd done before he attacked her. But there were no cows in view at all. And that was probably why Tammy thought she had a chance of getting to Bob. This was crazy! What had she created?

She lost sight of the motorcycle for a moment as it disappeared over the ridge. Then, topping the hill, her heart stopped and she screamed at the sight before her.

From one direction Sylvester was charging straight at the motorcycle! And from the opposite direction, Bob, always the hero, was running full out to intercept him.

And this time he didn't have his whip. Or his truck.

CHAPTER NINE

Lacy brought the Caddy to a jolting halt on top of the hill. "Molly, she's fixing to get Bob killed. And herself!"

Molly's heart was in her throat and she could only nod and keep on nodding, as she was forced to watch Bob charging toward the bull.

The foolish Tammy, realizing what was coming at her, at least had the good sense to attempt avoiding a head-on collision. Yanking her bike to the right, she sent gravel flying, but the back tire lost grip and spun out from under her. Now on its side, it was sliding with rider attached straight at Sylvester. Worse, Bob was closing in on certain destruction as the bike came to a halt with the rider beside it.

Seconds before Sylvester plowed into the prone figure, Bob sprang over the bike, placing himself directly between the crazed bull and crazier woman.

Quick on his feet, Bob slapped Sylvester's nose and did a pivot away from the bike, effectively drawing the bull's attention to himself. But there was nowhere for him to go! If they'd been in an arena, there would have been men to pick up the injured bull rider that Bob was trained to protect and there would have been a fence to climb over or a barrel to dive into once he'd risked his life to keep the bull from harming the bull rider. But he was in an open field. Alone.

"We have to do something," Molly and Lacy practically cried at the same time. Both of them knew this was no rodeo and Bob was in a losing battle with a bull that, Molly understood only too well, had no compulsion to quit.

"We're going after him." Lacy hit the gas and the horn at the same time. The Caddy jumped forward, ready to tango just as Sylvester lowered his massive head and went in for the kill.

Lacy and Molly were screaming at the top of their lungs praying that God would spare Bob and set the bull on them. But they were too far away to stop the inevitable and had to watch as the bull caught Bob full force. The only saving grace was Bob's quickness as he twisted, tagged the bull's forehead with his outstretched hand and used the stiff-armed action to propel himself to the side, spinning out of the way. It was a spectacular move, one Molly was sure he'd used as a diversionary tactic in the arena. But the massive bull merely twisted and continued after him, muscles rippling and bunching in powerful determination. Despite his effort, Bob took the next hit and Molly was forced to watch helplessly as he was trampled beneath the bull's hooves!

The Caddy was on the move, but still it seemed to Molly they would never get there. And all the while Sylvester was pummeling Bob into the earth.

"I'm going to try and draw him to the car, away from Bob," Lacy shouted, beating on the horn. Molly would have thrown herself out of the car and let the maniac trample her if it had meant getting him off Bob. But Lacy zipped past the bull.

"Please let him come after us. Please let him come after us," Molly chanted, all too aware of how much he hated cars. "I think he's attracted to moving targets," she called, relieved when Sylvester looked up and charged at the Caddy. Molly had already unsnapped her seat belt so she hopped to her knees, facing the back of the car waving her arms. "He's coming, Lacy, and I can see Bob moving. He's on the ground, but if we can give him enough time, maybe he can get himself and Tammy to safety. I've seen bull riders on TV get up after attacks like that." And she had. She didn't know how, but bull riders and bullfighters walked away from this kind of thing all the time. She could only pray this was one of those times.

"I'm going to follow the road around the house and see if we can get him over there. Maybe he'll pass out from exhaustion," Lacy yelled, driving like a pro, guiding the big car over rutted ground back onto the gravel road. *"Molly, a puppy!"* she suddenly screamed.

Molly whirled around, her gaze following Lacy's finger pointing to a ball of fur scurrying under the fence that protected the house from the open pasture. "Sylvester will kill it," Molly snapped. Her decision made, she glanced back at the bull that was only about twenty feet behind them. "Stop."

Lacy—bless her soul—didn't give it a moment's hesitation before she slammed on the breaks. Molly sprang over the door before the car came to a jarring halt. Feeling like an Olympian and praying for that kind of speed, Molly raced the five feet to the puppy and scooped it up with one hand. When she turned around, Lacy was there with the car already moving and Molly fell over the door face-first into safety.

Her relief was short-lived as she scrambled to her knees in the backseat to see Sylvester with his head down about to ram the back end of the Caddy.

HOLD ME, COWBOY

"Hang on," Lacy yelled, and floored it.

In the next instant they were trucking down the gravel road that circled past the house, around behind the barn, and into wide-open spaces. Madder than ever, Sylvester was pounding along right behind them. His head was still down like the grill guard of a train. He raged after them, hooves thundering beneath him.

Molly glanced at the black-and-brown puppy on the floorboard of the car, feeling relief that at least she'd saved Bob's dog. But what about Bob?

"Hey, Molly, there's a fence and an open gate. Hang on, we're going through."

Looking over her shoulder, Molly saw the gate. She had never been so happy to see anything in all her life. "Let's get him through then we can swing back around and I'll lock him in and hope he's bored with us and doesn't feel like knocking the fence down." She started waving her arms again, knowing she was closer to getting back to Bob and Tammy.

"Come on, you big brute," she yelled when he slowed. "Now is not the time to get bored with us. Just a little bit farther." They made it past the gate, but he was only trotting now, looking from side to side like a majestic powerhouse bored with his morning jog. When he pranced on through the gate, Molly wanted to cry with relief. She'd been preparing to jump out of the car and use herself as bait to draw him through if she'd needed to.

Instead, she was so relieved to see him follow them, she was cheering and jumping in the seat. When Lacy hit a hole, she almost flew out.

"Oops, sorry," Lacy called. "Molly, there are some more cows out there. I'll go in that direction to lead him away from the gate."

To Molly's great relief, Sylvester saw the cows, too, and trotted away from pursuing the car. "Hallelujah! Praise the Lord," she cried.

Seeing their opportunity, Lacy wasted no time. She wheeled the big car around and headed back to the gate, where Molly made short order of getting it pulled shut. Her hands were shaking as her thoughts riveted back to Bob and Tammy. She fumbled with the chain, finally secured it, then once again dove into the car.

All she could think about now were the two people lying in the pasture.

How bad were they hurt?

When the car rounded the curve, Molly could see Tammy standing up, looking at Bob.

Bob—who lay exactly where he'd been when Sylvester had mowed him down.

The hospital waiting room was packed and Molly was

about to pull all her hair out, her nerves were so shattered. This day had put ten years on her, easy. When they'd rounded the corner and had seen that Tammy was up but Bob was still down, she and Lacy had split up. Lacy went for the house and the phone to call 911 and Molly had run to Bob. He had been attempting to get up, which at least gave her a small touch of hope. But he'd been struggling, and his back had been bleeding through the shredded fabric of his shirt. Tammy had stripped off her helmet and, miraculously, probably due to all the leather she wore, she didn't seem hurt. But she was scared and kept repeating she hadn't meant to hurt him.

Molly had never felt so helpless in her life as she did when she sank into the grass beside Bob and eased him back down.

He'd taken one look at her and passed out.

But not before Molly had seen the look in his eyes. The accusing look.

The look that said he knew this was all her fault.

Tammy must have thought he was dead, because she had run over and picked up her bike and hopped on it. She'd just gotten it started and made it to the cattle guard when Brady pulled his big truck into the driveway and blocked her escape.

After that everything had happened fast. The rural

ambulance used the school that was twenty miles away as its wait station, and with Mule Hollow's lack of traffic, it took them just a little over fifteen minutes to reach them. By that time Bob had awakened and was angry as a hornet. She'd been applying pressure to a nasty laceration on his shoulder with a towel Brady had given her. But Bob had demanded in no uncertain terms that she get away from him.

The demand out, he'd promptly passed out again and Brady had put her back to applying pressure to his wound while he stabilized Bob's neck.

She'd never prayed so much in her entire life. She was still praying.

Tammy hadn't sustained any injury and she'd wasted no time hopping back on her motorcycle and heading out of town. After the strident warning she'd received from Brady, Molly didn't think Bob would have to worry about ever seeing crazy Tammy again. He would probably be more relieved if he never saw Molly again. She deserved his scorn. She still couldn't believe she'd been directly responsible for nearly getting him killed. But it was true. And he knew it.

"How are you holding up?" Norma Sue asked, coming up beside her and handing her a cup of coffee.

Her lip trembling, Molly stared at the coffee and felt the heat of tears burn behind her eyes and the ache in her chest from all the pressure of fighting them off. She wouldn't cry anymore. Tears wouldn't do Bob any good. And she didn't want sympathy from anyone. She was to blame.

"When I became a reporter," she managed to get out at last, her voice sounding weak even to her own ears, "I never thought about someone actually being harmed because of something I wrote. I...I don't like this. I'm not doing well at all. What if Bob dies? Of all the irresponsible things...I feel dirty. I feel like I've been writing for one of those trash magazines."

Norma Sue startled her by wrapping an arm around her waist and giving her a gentle hug. "Bob isn't going to die. He's pretty banged up, but he's a tough one. Don't you know that cowboys are made of stiff stuffing and rubber bones? It'd take more than a little trampling to put one under. Especially that one."

"But you should have seen it, Norma. It was terrible. He could be dead right now."

"But he's not, Molly," Lacy said, coming down the hall from the room where Bob was being stitched up. "That's right," Norma continued. "He's okay. Like I was telling you, he's got a hairline fracture in his leg—which won't require anything but an orthopedic boot—and several busted ribs and a herd of bruises. But honey, his spine is fine and his internal organs aren't damaged. At least they don't think so. They're going to keep him overnight to observe him, since these things aren't that easily detected. But mostly it's his pride that's damaged. Knowing Bob, he thought he could out dance that bull. You know he was one of the best bullfighters in the industry when he quit. There's a lot of bull riders out there who owe him their lives."

Molly took a steadying breath and nodded. "I read about him on the Internet a few weeks ago."

"Then you know he's been through a lot worse than this."

"Yes. But *I'm* the cause of this."

Norma met her gaze. The older woman's plump face suddenly lifted as she smiled the huge smile that spread almost as wide as her ears were apart. "Then you should make amends. Ain't that right, Lacy? He is going to be pretty stove up."

"Yep," Lacy chirped, and clapped her hands together. "That would be the perfect thing. Poor Bob has no one around here to look after him. And with his ribs all smashed and his leg in that walking boot, it will be hard for him to get around. Not to mention someone will need to look after his puppy."

Norma Sue was nodding agreement with every word that Lacy spewed out and Molly could hear the lightbulb exploding in their heads. Shameless, just shameless, that's what they were, but they were right! And the thought of actually helping Bob after all the trouble she'd caused him this past week was overwhelming in the relief it gave her.

"I'll do it. I can cook for him and clean. And I will just pamper him so he has to forgive me. I'm already taking care of his cute little puppy."

Lacy and Norma Sue were all grins.

She pulled to her full height, shoulders back, spine stiff...she was going to help him. Then she deflated. "But he told me to stay away from him. You heard him. He wasn't nice at all."

The memory of the scene only a couple of hours ago had put a stake in her heart when she'd tried to see him in the emergency room. His harsh words had stopped her at the door. He'd told her she'd been nothing but trouble to him from the moment she'd entered Mule Hollow and taken it upon herself to ramrod his life. Ramrod! Is that what she'd done? Would that be what she was doing now?

He might not want to see her, but she had to stay.

Had to make certain he was okay.

"You aren't going to let a little bad temper stop you, are you?" Norma Sue asked.

"That's right," Lacy added, moving to stand closer. "He got hit on the head pretty good. Probably knocked him bonkers, so he didn't know what he was saying. You know how mild mannered Bob is, how nice and considerate he is. Of course when sparks are flying, people tend not to be themselves."

"Stop with the sparks." Molly groaned. If there had ever been the slightest hint that Bob may have been attracted to her it was gone now. "I want to help him to make up for the bad things I caused to happen to him. And that's it."

Norma Sue nodded so hard that her gray curls danced around on top of her head. "We understand. Don't we, Lacy?"

"You bet we do. And we will do whatever we need to do to help make it happen."

That was what Molly was worried about. But at this point she needed so much to make up to Bob, she didn't really care what was going on in her friends' heads.

Yes, it was to assuage her guilt, she admitted.

And yes, she felt terrible about that. But it was the right thing to do.

She nodded her head to finalize the deal with herself and then she stood up straight again. She could do this. She might have gotten Bob into this mess, but there was no way she was going to leave him to suffer alone.

"How mad do you think he's going to get?"

Norma laughed and slapped her on the back. "Men, they get mad, but they straighten up pretty fast. Besides, I haven't met one yet that doesn't need a little prodding from the female population. He's going to come around. Especially if you take real good care of that puppy."

Looking from Norma Sue to Lacy, Molly knew she'd walked straight into a setup. But what was she to do? Well, this was one setup she was going to be in control of from the beginning. The matchmaking ladies of Mule Hollow could just rewind their ideas about her and Bob Jacobs being another happily-ever-after. Even if they couldn't see it, Molly had eyes, and if there were ever two people who were night and day to each other it was them.

And besides, she was so in hopes that she was about to get the call she'd been waiting on all of her life. She was glad she'd decided to take the plunge and send those résumés out while she was a hot commodity. A girl had to ride the wave while the tide was rolling, and the way she was feeling about things right now, the sooner something opened up for her the better. Well, at least, she meant as soon as was possible after she made up to Bob the wrong that she'd done to him. Just remembering the look in his eyes before he'd passed out was enough to make her do whatever it took to make him…to make him what? Like her? Respect her again? What was she wanting from him? Forgiveness? Or was it more?

She shook off the questions. This had nothing to do with what she wanted from him. It had to do simply with helping him through a tough time.

That she'd instigated.

Clint hit a bump in the road and Bob felt every muscle in his body protest.

"Sorry, buddy," Clint said, glancing over at him.

"I'll live," Bob said, bracing his ribs with his arm.

He was glad to be out of the hospital. It was strange, only a week ago he'd been saving Molly from Sylvester. It seemed like forever. "So y'all got Sylvester fixed up?"

"We loaded him up and put him way out in the back section of my ranch where the big monster can cool off. Like you said, he's so agitated right now we don't need to take any more chances of him getting at anyone else. He won't be seeing anyone way out there."

"Thanks. It's a wonder he didn't kill someone. He

developed a real burr in his bonnet when it came to the sound of that motorcycle. I should have moved him after I noticed how irritated he acted whenever that woman stopped down at the gate."

"Bob, the bull was on your property. She had no right to cross that cattle guard."

Clint spoke the truth. Still, that didn't stop the guilt he felt at knowing two people had almost been harmed because of his bull. Sylvester had always been high-strung. But he'd never acted this wild before. Then again Bob had never seen so much madness in all of his life.

"You were pretty hard on Molly yesterday," Clint said, his voice more inquiring than censuring.

Bob would have raked his hand through his hair in frustration if he'd been able to lift his arm, but his shoulder was banged up pretty bad and it was impossible. At least for today. He knew from experience that it would take a few days for his body to get over the beating it had taken. It might take a little longer to get over what was going on inside his head when it came to thinking about Molly.

Reporters, they spun their stories without a second thought about whom they were hurting in the process. "She got what she deserved." He hated the way saying that made him feel. Yeah, he was angry. Angrier than he'd been since the day his dad had walked away and left him at the boarding school, without a backward glance. "Look, Clint. This was insane. I know I'm supposed to forgive Molly for the trouble she's caused me. But right now, I'm just not up to it. I'm dry."

He needed some time alone. He wanted to get home, close the door and listen to the silence of his home. He was mad, frustrated and guilt ridden—which he was a little confused about. Why should he be guilty?

Immediately his thoughts went to Molly's expression when he'd told her in no uncertain terms to get out of the emergency room. He'd hurt her.

And just why should that bother him? She'd almost gotten him killed.

"Brace yourself," Clint warned as he turned into Bob's driveway and started over the cattle guard.

Bob gritted his teeth, which was about the only part of his body he could move well enough to brace. The sharp, ruthless pain that jackknifed through his ribs stole his breath, forcing him to fight off a groan. His body wasn't what it used to be, that was for certain.

"Glad I don't have any more of those to go over." Clint gave him an apologetic grin after they crossed the second cattle guard, separating Bob's yard from the pasture.

Bob was able to grit out, "Yeah," feeling every bounce of the truck as it eased up the driveway toward his house.

He was more than ready to exit the truck and enter the solitude and peace of his home.

Molly's newly repainted yellow VW Bug sitting behind his truck at the back of his house wasn't the call to relaxation he was hoping for.

CHAPTER TEN

Be calm, Molly. It was easier said than done, Molly thought, stepping out onto Bob's back porch. She watched Clint's black truck pull to a halt behind her Bug and wondered what had possessed her to even think she should do this!

She closed her eyes and lifted her hand from her rolling stomach to pet the puppy she cradled in her other arm. If the good Lord had any pity on her at all, He'd call her home to glory right then and there and spare her the trauma of what was about to happen.

You can do this, Molly. She sucked in a calming breath, and almost choked on the air because there was no moisture in her throat. And even if there had been, as she stepped forward and glimpsed the shell-shocked expression on Bob's face when he spotted her, there was no way a measly little breath of air was going to stop the pounding of her heart or the sweat that started dripping from her armpits.

If she'd ever thought she was one of those dainty little women who didn't sweat, well, she wasn't. She was a dripping mess. Inside and out.

This wasn't about her, though. That thought was the only thing that made her step forward. She knew from the get-go that Bob wasn't going to welcome her with open arms—even if the poor guy could open his arms. No matter how uncomfortable she might be, or how rude he might get, she wasn't throwing in the towel, because she deserved every bit of his hostility. After all, the angry man staring at her was one she had created. This man was not the Bob she'd watched month after month and had come to admire.

No, that wasn't right, either. Nice guys could get angry. She hadn't put him up on a pedestal. No, she'd hit a nerve in Bob that she'd not realized was there. Something she had to fix. And no matter what it took, she was going to fix it.

Lifting her chin and holding the now-squirming puppy with both hands, she walked forward and opened the truck door.

"What are you doing here?" he growled.

She'd read an article on writing once that said people didn't growl. She begged to differ. This was growling, and it was so out of place on Bob that it cut right to her heart.

The harsh words had her stepping back despite having prepared herself for his anger. "I'm here to take care of you. And your puppy." And she could. She really could. She would find a way to put the sparkle back into Bob's beautiful eyes.

"I can take care of myself." He continued, "Believe me. I don't need your kind of help."

His navy eyes raked her up and down, as if he hoped to freeze her with their icy coldness. For a moment Molly couldn't speak. What had she done? This wasn't the sweet Bob she'd known. This cowboy was as hard as they came. The only softness she glimpsed was when his eyes rested on the puppy that was obviously glad to see him by the way he was squirming to get out of her arms and get to his master. Blinking away the need to cry, Molly held on to the puppy, and reached inside herself to drag up some frost of her own.

She was staying.

She owed it to him whether he wanted it or not. If tough love was what he needed, tough love was what he would get. "I got you into this mess and I'm going to get you out of it. And there isn't anything you can do to stop me, so forget about it."

HOLD ME, COWBOY

"Clint, tell this woman I don't need a nursemaid." Clint shook his head, his eyes light with humor.

"Well, Bob, as a matter of fact, the doctor said you did. At least for a week minimum. 'Seven days' were his exact words, when the stitches come out. He said that living out here in the boondocks all by yourself could pose a problem. That he at least wants someone with you during the day."

"I don't care what the doc said. She's not looking after me. Or John Boy."

Molly slammed her free fist to her hip and glared at him. "I am. Someone needs to change the dressings on all those lacerations and someone needs to feed you and John Boy."

Clint strode around to Bob's side and helped him maneuver out of the truck. Molly was horrified at how slowly he had to move. The way he sagged slightly against Clint's side was a good indicator of the extent of his pain. She had pulled up articles on the Internet about bullfighters and injuries. One of them said getting run over by a bull was like being run over by a car going twenty miles an hour. Watching the excruciatingly slow movements as Bob held on to Clint as they negotiated the steps brought back the sting of tears.

Focus, Molly. Focus. Remember why you're here.

You are here to earn his forgiveness. You are here to make amends. You are not here to cry all over his manly feelings. Men do not like sympathy!

Walking up the steps behind them, she wiped her eyes with her fingertips, tightened her gut muscles and dared herself to cry again. She could do this. With God's help, she could do anything.

"I fixed some potato soup," she said brightly, placing John Boy in the pen beside the steps. "Esther Mae gave me the recipe and said it's really good for sick people. So I gave it a whirl." She tried to make her voice light but didn't do a passable job. John Boy whined and yapped his displeasure at being left outside. Molly wanted to go back out and join him but held fast to her determination.

"I'm not sick and I don't need you cooking for me. Go home, Molly."

Again she pushed away the need to run. *I can do all things through Christ, who strengthens me.* Yes, she could.

"Stop your growling, cowboy. You need me."

"Clint, don't—and I mean *do not*—let this woman stay. Escort her out as you leave."

Clint chuckled as he carefully helped Bob sit down on the large sofa, undoubtedly not the easiest transition for someone with cracked ribs. The poor guy was sweating bullets, even grunting despite his attempt to pretend he had everything under control. And he didn't think he needed her. Ha!

"Sorry, buddy," Clint said, cutting off his chuckles. "I'm stayin' out of this one. Lacy gave me strict orders."

Molly noticed he made sure he was out of swinging range when he made that statement. Not that Bob could have swung anything. He opted instead to ram the couch with his elbow. A movement he immediately regretted, if the expression on his face was any meter to read.

Clint backed up. "It'll be okay, Bob. Call me if you need me." Then he spun on his boot heel and headed for the door.

"Clint! Don't you leave."

If eyes could throw daggers, Clint's back would have been covered in them as he made for the door, chuckling all the way.

Molly covered her mouth with her hand to cover her quivering lips. She'd learned from her time in Mule Hollow that cowboys would be boys, despite any discomfort they might be feeling or inflicting.

The door closed and suddenly she was alone with Bob. And she got the distinct feeling that even Sylvester wouldn't want to tango with him at this moment.

That being the case, she chose the safety of the kitchen. Figuring food might be the way to a calmer man, she poured him a glass of tea and dished him up a bowl of soup. She could see the back of his head from the kitchen stove and was not surprised that he didn't move an inch. He sat as rigid and unyielding as a statue. Her nerves poked a head out of hiding and she prayed for the right things to do. To say.

Then she picked up the tray. "Okay, Molly, here we go. Doc gave you a week to make things right," she whispered out loud. Tightening her gut again and hardening her resolve, she blew out a breath to stabilize her nerves.

It didn't work.

"What are you doing, Molly?" Through slit eyes, Bob watched Molly set a tray on the table in front of him. He tried to ignore the dark circles under her eyes and the vulnerable wavering that flickered through them.

"Look, Bob." She let go of the tray, then placed her hands on her lean hips. "Admit it, you know you need help. You can't even get off the couch by yourself. And remember someone needs to look after John Boy."

She was right about that, but he kept his mouth shut. The woman had done enough to mess things up for him. All he had to do was sniff the air to know what was in his dining room.

He studied her—the graceful line of her jaw, the tension that was starkly out of place there as she reached for the necklace around her neck. He'd come to know the action meant she was nervous or unsure.

There was at least some satisfaction that he was making her nervous.

"I brought you some soup and some tea. I know you're hurting. You're going to need to take a pain pill. And the doctor sent some antibiotics, too. Those cuts on your shoulder are deep."

"How do you know what I'm supposed to be taking?"

"Well, I spoke to a nurse about it. I am taking care of you."

He shook his head and stared at the floor. The toe of her shoe was in his peripheral vision and he watched as she ground it on the rug before plopping to her knees in front of him. Placing her hands on her thighs, she looked up at him.

"Come on, Bob. I know I messed up. I know I goofed your life up." She swallowed hard and blinked back tears. *Tears.* "I know you hate me, but I'm not running out on you. Yes, I understand everyone would come over here and take care of you if I left. But they're giving me a chance to prove that I'm sorry. And even if you don't want me here, you have to admit that I'm the one who should be. S-since this is my fault."

He hated tears. And he hated feeling like a jerk. And he knew he was acting like one despite all the reasons he could use as an excuse to get away with it.

He looked away from her, fighting the sudden need to pull her close and tell her everything was okay. Not that he could do that. He only had half a good arm at the moment and its range of motion wasn't that great since it was bandaged to the hilt and stitched even further.

There was no denying that she was right about him not being able to get off the couch. And there was John Boy to think about.

Still, tears or no tears, he didn't need to be entertaining any thoughts about comforting Molly. Looking at her bright eyes, he suddenly felt like a doomed man.

"All right, you can stay. But don't baby me," he said gruffly. Her smile told him she'd completely ignored the gruff part.

"No babying. Honest."

His stomach growled and he had to give in and nod toward the soup. "So how does it taste?" Anything had to be better than what little he'd eaten at the hospital.

"I'll let you tell me," she chirped a little too brightly. Grabbing the bowl, she held it out to him.

Bob ignored the initial pain that shot from his elbow up to his shoulder as he reached for the bowl. He grimaced despite himself. The stiffness and the pain were going to make lifting a spoon and holding a bowl difficult. In the hospital a nurse had tried to feed him and he'd refused to eat that way, so consequently he was starving now. He reached for the bowl again only to have Molly snatch it back. The look in her eyes sent dread rushing through him.

"How could I have been so thoughtless? You can't maneuver a spoon, not with your shoulder like it is."

He lifted an eyebrow. "I'll figure something out. Give me the bowl." He wiggled his fingers for the bowl, not certain what he would do once she gave it to him. She shook her head. "Come on, Molly, give me the bowl." He didn't like the look in her eyes as she glanced from him to the bowl.

He didn't like it one bit.

Molly eyed Bob. What in the world had she been thinking?

News flash—she hadn't been! As a matter of fact, the soup had been Esther Mae and Norma Sue's idea, now that Molly was thinking about it. Why of all the sneaky shenanigans! They didn't miss a beat. They were excellent at what they did. Molly had to give it to them, those dedicated women of the Mule Hollow Matchmaking Brigade. They just picked a pair of poor suckers and went after them, even knowing there was no way in the world this would work. Of course, she realized her being here probably took a lot of the heat off of them going after Sam and Adela.

Holding in a sigh of stupidity, she moved to perch on the arm of the couch. Bob looked at her doubtfully as she dipped the spoon into the soup. "I know you're in pain. But the movement of lifting this spoon up and down is just going to aggravate the injuries. And that's even if you could figure out a way to do it."

He didn't say anything, only looked from the spoon to her face. She made slow circles in the air with the spoon, hoping to show that it was not the evil his expression implied. In the end his hunger won the battle and he opened his mouth.

"When the swelling goes down some and the stitches come out it'll be easier to move. The doctor said you were lucky not to have two broken collarbones and broken arms to go along with the ribs. That's one reason you're so sore in the upper area of your shoulders. He said—"

"I know what he said, Molly. I was there, remember."

She felt the heat of a blush as it rose from her toes and hit her hairline. The room was suddenly uncomfortably quiet as she concentrated on loading up the spoon and willed her hand not to shake. She swallowed the uncertainty that threatened to take away her determination. What had made her think this would work? If he didn't want her here—

"This isn't half bad."

Molly lifted her eyes and met his. Clearly he was offering her an olive branch. She smiled. It wasn't compliance, but it was something. It was a glimpse of the easygoing, charming guy. The one she could be at ease with. Well, at least she could pretend better with the mild-mannered guy versus the intense guy.

She smiled and willed the flutters in her chest to go away. "We'll see what you say later. There's bacon grease in it and cheese galore. I can't exactly figure out why Norma Sue said it was healthy when it's full of all kinds of no-no's."

His stomach growled as if it was on steroids and he lifted his chin toward the hovering spoon. "I'll take my chances."

He smiled, and for the first time in days his dimples showed.

Molly's heart missed a beat. Oh but the man had to-die-for dimples.

She suddenly had to wonder if she was as daft as everyone had pegged her. Bob was the perfect man and she was trying to pawn him off on someone else. The stack of envelopes in his dining room had been clamoring for her attention since she'd walked into his home. And now, looking at his dimples, she had to wonder about those letters.

At first she hadn't seen them because of the way the formal-style dining area was separated by a wall from the more open kitchen and great room. However, the malodorous smell wafting from the doorway had pressed her reporter button and drawn her to see if her nose was telling the truth. Were there a hundred women crammed into Bob's dining room? Women who obviously hadn't read the memo about perfume! Or was there something else going on behind that wall? The scent was ghastly to say the least.

It had looked like a mound of giant-size confetti, and her fingers had immediately itched to open a few of the letters. Well, the scent kind of made her itch all over, adding to her impatience to see exactly what kind of correspondence she'd garnered for him. They couldn't all be weird wackos despite how they smelled. And deep inside, despite how abysmal she felt about

HOLD ME, COWBOY

having caused this unfortunate situation for Bob, she was still curious. She was a reporter, after all.

But they were Bob's letters, not hers, to read. To smell, but not to read. So she hadn't read any.

Yet.

And here she was wondering why she was trying to give him away and not fighting for his attentions herself.

She realized he was watching her, waiting as she let the spoonful of soup float between them.

"You zoned out on me."

"Sorry. I was thinking." She offered the spoon.

"About?" the word came out muffled as he chewed on a potato.

"The letters," she squeaked. "Have you read any of them?" She knew it was a bad thing to bring up, but her curiosity always got her in trouble. She cringed as his scowl slammed into place. "Sorry. I was just curious. I mean true, Tammy was a little off-the-wall. And yes, the others, too. But Bob, think about it—there could be some really nice letters in there." She plunged onward, reminding herself that career came first so she had to stop letting all this matchmaking talk go to her head.

"Forget it, Molly. I'm as likely to read the letters as I am to sign up for one of those online dating services."

"Hey, I happen to know several friends back in

Houston who had great luck with online dating."

"Really." Total disbelief sounded in his voice.

"Yes, really. And that guy on TV says things are great—"

"And I'm really happy for him. But don't get any ideas about signing me up. Thank you very much, you've done enough."

The look he gave her said *no debate.* So they were at a standoff. She lifted another spoonful of soup and held it out to him like a peace offering.

After a second he took it. A man's growling stomach obviously overrode irritation.

"Could I read a few?" she asked, hoping he didn't bite her head off. "I mean, really, Bob, they did take the time to write them."

"Molly, you can read as many as you want as long as you promise to throw them away so I don't have to smell them anymore. And as long as you promise not to read any of them to me."

She rammed the spoon into the bowl and stared at him. "But, let's just examine the possibility that your Miss Right is in there. It could happen. Like in the movies—"

"Believe me, Molly, I've seen the movies and there is no way I'm going to the top of the Empire State Building or anywhere else. So forget it."

Molly held her tongue and offered another bite of soup. She wasn't exactly sure what her problem was, but the fact that he was so closed minded wasn't helping.

Besides, God could have used her to bring him together with his one true love.

Even if the thought suddenly settled in her stomach like a lump of lard.

"Molly, read my lips. Forget about it. You got that? Forget about it."

Bob was sleeping. Knocked out actually. Molly had fed him and gotten his single cowboy boot off. After much tugging, she'd realized there was an art to getting off a boot. She was not an artist, but she'd finally managed it without crippling his good foot. Then she'd helped him prop both feet on the end of the couch, cringing herself as she'd watched him slide into a reclining position on the sofa. It had been horribly painful. It had assured her that she never wanted to experience broken ribs herself. Finally, when the pain medication had started to take effect, she'd brought in John Boy and held him away from Bob's ribs as he petted the wriggling puppy. She found it adorable the way he'd talked to the puppy like a baby.

After the medicine caused Bob to drift into painless slumber, she'd covered him with a lightweight blanket then almost broken her own neck getting to the hoard of mail!

"Where do I start?" she asked the puppy sitting in her lap. He seemed to be studying the pile, too. He sneezed as if to say stop dillydallying and just do it! So she did.

She closed her eyes and reached for one, an odd combination of anticipation and dread taking hold of her. When she opened her eyes, she was clutching a pink envelope with kisses all over it.

"Oh, John Boy, how cheesy is that! Didn't these women read my column? Don't they know that's not Bob?" There was no sense opening one she knew right off the bat wouldn't be right for Bob, so she dropped it to the floor, closed her eyes and grabbed again.

This time she peeped through one eye and was relieved to see a tasteful blue envelope, devoid of any garish adornment. "Okay, now we're talking." The newspaper hadn't given out Bob's physical address. Instead the letters were addressed to "Bob Jacobs, C/O General Delivery, Mule Hollow, Texas." She still had to force away her guilt as, her heart fluttering, she tore the first one open and started reading aloud.

And almost fell out of her chair!

HOLD ME, COWBOY

"Whoa! John Boy, cover your ears baby." She glared at the words on the paper. Brother, could looks be deceiving!

"*Soap.* That's what this woman needs, John Boy," she gasped. The puppy was looking up at her with curious eyes. "What was she thinking to write *that?*"

Feeling really cheap, Molly folded the offensive letter, fumbling while cramming it back in the envelope. She glanced at the kissy-lipped one. Maybe it might be better—nah. She just couldn't go there.

She opted instead for a red one with hearts all over it. Thinking positive, she tore it open.

Dear Bob, I've been reading Molly's column from the very beginning and must say that you have impressed me very much. If Molly thinks you are so wonderful, then I'm sure it must be true. So I would love to meet...

Molly stopped reading. She sounded decent, maybe sweet. Feeling like an interloper, she folded the letter back up and placed it on her right side, away from the other letters on her left, which she would call the No-Way-In-My-Lifetime-Pal pile. It hit her then that she wasn't an interloper; she was Bob's advocate.

Yes. That was exactly what she was!

Which meant she had a serious job to do. Molly scanned the pile more intently, a sense of purpose replacing some of the guilt she'd been feeling. She'd come here to make up to Bob for what had turned into a circus. But, if Miss Right was in that pile, then it was up to Molly to find her and give her the chance she deserved. The chance Bob deserved.

John Boy barked and grinned up at her as if sensing she'd hit upon the truth, telling her this meant business. Indeed it did. Molly ran a hand down the puppy's back, sucked in a cleansing breath, expelled all the negative doubts and misgivings. Coughing on the smell, she reached for another letter.

"'Dear Bob, have you ever seen the movie *Sleepless in Seattle?*'" Molly laughed out loud and tossed the letter to the left. "Sorry, girlfriend, *nooo* Empire State Buildings for Bob."

CHAPTER ELEVEN

Molly had long since put John Boy in his pen after it became obvious by his sneezes that it wasn't good for him to be around the letters. Her back was cramping and she was in the middle of a huge sneeze herself when she heard Bob say something. Glad for a reason to get up, she laid down the letter in her hand and went to see what he needed. But when she entered the room he was silent.

"Bob," she said softly, bending over him. He looked so tranquil with his eyes closed, his dark lashes feathering across his tanned skin. An unruly lock of hair had fallen across his forehead and, before she could stop herself, she touched the curl.

She'd always admired his hair, its dark rich waves. They were as silky to touch as she'd thought they would be. Biting her lip, she very lightly brushed it back from his forehead, glad that the crease of pain had relaxed. There was so much about Bob that was almost too good to be true. But she'd been around him long enough to know everything about Bob Jacobs was real. He was beautiful. Inside and out…

He shifted slightly and his nose twitched, probably from the residue of perfume hovering about her like a cloud.

"Bob, what can I do for you?" she asked again, but he was obviously asleep. He mumbled and she smiled. Yep. Just what she'd suspected—he was talking in his sleep. Curiosity got the better of her and she leaned forward. Her long hair fell from her shoulder and settled on his chin. Immediately his eyes flew open and she was caught red-handed hovering over him, staring straight into his dark eyes.

"Hello, beautiful," he said woozily.

She froze. Just froze, her face right there two inches from trouble! Her heart thundered like the thud of a thousand horses' hooves on hard dirt.

Move, Molly girl. Step away from the cowboy!

"H-hello," she finally managed breathlessly, continuing to hover like a hovercraft. Incapable of movement.

Bob's dreamy gaze roved from her stunned eyes to her lips. Her eyes responded by seeking his lips. They were perfect lips. Wide and smooth with an upward tilt at the edges, as if he was always on the verge of a smile. That was Bob. At least, that used to be Bob, before she'd messed up his life.

"I...I thought you needed me," she said at last. Snapping to her senses, she stood and pushed her hair behind her ears. Fleeing would be good.

But she couldn't. He was smiling up at her and that was far stronger than the pull of escape. Besides, it was obvious that the painkillers were in full effect.

"I do need you."

Molly laughed, feeling foolishly giddy at his words. It was the medication at work on his brain, she knew this. Still, the sensation the words ignited in her heart was startlingly real. Molly stepped back as if she'd touched a hot skillet. But his grunt of discomfort when he suddenly struggled to sit up drew her right back to the frying pan.

No! She dropped to her knees. "Here, let me help you," she gasped, reaching for him. He paused, smiling lazily at her with the dopey smile of someone not in their right mind.

"That'd be mighty kind of you," he drawled. His lids heavy, his expression slack, he studied her, leaning forward then pulling back. "Feels like my middle got broke," he grunted, but struggled again to straighten up.

"Wait!" she cried again. His face crinkled in pain, he watched her grab two pillows from the floor where she'd set them when Clint had first brought him home. Gently she wrapped an arm behind his good shoulder, or at least his best shoulder, trying to miss his patchwork of stitches. "Okay, easy now," she coaxed, taking some of his weight as he shifted enough for her to slip a pillow behind him.

Their faces were close. She could actually feel his hair against her forehead as she gently helped him ease into a more comfortable position, all the while well aware of his breath on her cheek.

The kiss came out of nowhere.

One minute she was helping him lean back and the next moment he tilted his head downward and met her lips with his. Molly's entire thought process exploded with shock.

And then as quickly as it happened it was over. It really couldn't even be classified as a real kiss it ended so quickly. By the time she'd realized he was actually kissing her and she'd opened her eyes—eyes she hadn't remembered closing—it was done. And it was like payback for all the trouble she'd caused him.

Serious payback. Because when she opened her eyes, Bob was asleep.

Peacefully, obliviously asleep. And Molly?

Well, Molly was a mess.

Bob lay awake in his bed and stared at the ceiling. Shadows of the tree limbs were dancing above him, illuminated from the bright moon. If he lay very still, he could relax and the aches of his body could be ignored.

Almost.

His thoughts returned to Molly. He'd given her a hard time, but like a trouper, she'd hung in there and was trying hard to make amends for the mess she'd created in his life.

He smiled. She was determined to take care of him. Sure, he knew part of it was to assuage her guilt, but he'd be lying if he didn't admit that, after the initial shock of her presence, he was glad to have her here. If she'd had any idea how badly he'd been beaten up in his lifetime, she would be stunned to know these injuries were nothing in comparison.

He felt a little guilty. He'd always lived through his injuries before and had managed fine alone. He knew the routine well. He would hurt something fierce for a few days and then he'd be fine. Bullfighting in the PBR wasn't ranked number three out of the top ten worst jobs a person could have for nothing. It was a tough business.

Some people didn't realize a rider faced a bull during a ride maybe twice on any given night, while a bullfighter faced as many as seventy bulls in that same event. It was a dangerous job, and pain and injury were part of it. It wasn't a job he missed.

At least not now. When he'd lived it, he'd loved it. Then he'd met the Lord on a long dark stretch of Texas road. On that night his perspective had changed on everything.

He'd been coming back from an event and he was worn out. He'd drifted to sleep behind the wheel—something he'd never done before—and he'd sideswiped a guardrail. Ironically, he put his life on the line in a single evening at work more times than five men combined would in a year—and it took a duel with a guardrail to wake him up. Not that the Lord hadn't been working on him for months, but he'd been stubborn. However, in that instant, when just a thin strip of metal had kept him from plunging into the Trinity River, the Lord in all His mercy and grace had stripped him bare.

God had prepared him for the meeting earlier that evening when Bob attended a church service held before the events started. The preacher had read a verse from the Third Book of Lamentations and it was that verse Bob was thinking of when he woke, his truck grinding down the side of the railing, bowing it out to the breaking point.

"The Lord is good to those whose hope is in Him, to the one who seeks Him."

Sitting on the side of the road that night, Bob had prayed for hope. He'd prayed that the Lord would take the chest full of anger and resentment he'd been carrying around since he was a kid and release him from it. When he'd driven away from the spot twenty minutes later, he'd been a changed man. First and foremost, he no longer walked alone. He'd felt God's presence the instant he'd asked Him into his heart. And God had replaced the anger and resentment with a rekindling of his childhood desire to have a family to call his own. Bob started looking for the right place to settle down the next day. Over the years he'd crisscrossed the country several times and had seen a lot of places. But now he was watching for a place to call his own. Making plans and seeking the right fit for his future, the right place to make a home. When he'd found Mule Hollow, he'd retired with no regrets.

And now he was waiting on the woman to make his dreams come true.

Ignoring the pain in his neck and shoulders, he rolled his head just enough to glance one more time at the clock and wish for daylight. It had been a very long night.

Before Molly had left for the evening, she had worked to help him up off the couch, but it wasn't happening. When your insides were all broken up, it was almost impossible to get to your feet from a reclining position. In the end he'd been forced to chuck his pride and show her how it was done. Which meant, rolling from a reclining position onto his hands and knees on the floor. Then, using the table for leverage, he had eased his way to a standing position. Yeah, it was a sad sight. But when you had a chest full of broke ribs, bending at the waist was almost worse than getting stomped on in the first place.

Of course, now that she'd seen him struggling his pride hurt just as bad. Not that it mattered what Molly thought of him.

Yeah right, cowboy. You keep telling yourself that. She'd smelled as good as a fresh spring day when she'd wrapped her arms around him and gently tried to ease his pain. It was just plain distracting.

When he'd finally made it to a standing position, she was tucked beneath his good arm, her face tilted back as she earnestly studied his face. And that's when it had happened. Her face was flushed a gentle pink and, well…he had the sudden urge to bend his head down and kiss her. Of course he blamed it on the medicine. Kissing Molly would be about as good an idea as going back out there and letting Sylvester finish him off.

It hadn't made things any better that she was looking up at him with the startled eyes of a deer caught in a headlight, like maybe she might have been thinking about kissing him, too.

Yeah, it was the medicine. It had addled his brain.

One look at the pencil behind her ear reminded him to get his act together. Molly Popp the reporter, was leaving Mule Hollow the minute the story was over and the next opportunity arrived. And just because being around her all day had brought back that initial attraction he'd felt for her, he had better batten down the hatches better.

Yep. That was what he'd been telling himself for the past five hours as he lay captive in his bed staring up at the ceiling.

He listened to the seconds tick by on his alarm clock. If he could raise his hand up without pain, he'd check his skull for concussions. Because there had to be something wrong with his brain. There had to be.

Fact was, despite all the reasons he had to be ticked off at Molly, all he could think about was her sweetness. That sweetness kept coming back to nudge away any anger he had for her.

She'd placed the cordless phone right beside his arm on the mattress just in case there was an emergency, checked all the fire-alarm batteries in case there was a fire while he slept...she wanted to make certain something alerted him in case of a fire.

She was sweet, all right. She'd spent all that time making certain he was as comfortable as possible, protected him from as much harm as she could and then she'd taken his dog and gone home.

He grinned. She'd gone home, completely forgetting to bring him his pain medicine before she left.

He felt the smile that spread across his face. If it didn't hurt so much, he would laugh. But when a guy had four broken ribs among other things, he did not laugh.

He didn't sleep, either.

What he did was a tubload of thinking.

Walking into Bob's silent kitchen, Molly set her purse on the tiled counter, set the puppy down to play and surveyed Bob's home once more. It was obvious by the things he'd surrounded himself with that he was going to be a wonderful family man. He'd set his roots deep in this house that he'd lived in for a little over a month. There was warmth in his home, which didn't surprise her, because there was a warmth to Bob. He'd decorated in creams and tans, adding splashes of reds and greens throughout. It wasn't magazine perfect, but it was close.

He had paintings on the walls and pillows on the chairs. There were large colorful rugs on the floors and even a beautiful arrangement of flowers in the entrance hall. Everything about this house said Welcome to my home. Bob Jacobs hadn't been kidding when he'd said he was ready for a wife. He was ready to fill his home with a family.

And he'd need the perfect wife for the perfect husband.

All the more reason for her get over the schoolgirl jitters she was having around the man.

Do you have feelings for Bob?

That question had stalked her all night. It was his fault, with that kiss! She hadn't signed on thinking about being kissed...didn't seem to matter that it had been a peck. It had messed her up so bad for the rest of the afternoon that she'd zipped around like a dizzy jabber-mouth, unable to look Bob in the eye without growing pink! He'd made her so nervous, watching her as she'd taken precautions to make sure he would be safe alone for the night. By the time she'd grabbed John Boy and fled, she'd been certain he thought she didn't have a brain.

"Do I have feelings for Bob?" she mumbled under her breath. It was foolish even toying with the idea. It had just been the surprise of the kiss…but then there was the way he'd said he needed her. Not that she believed it.

It was crazy, crazy, crazy.

And more crazy. He didn't need her—he'd been doped up on painkillers, for goodness' sakes.

She took a deep breath. She had to get a hold of herself—if she could find where the real Molly Popp had disappeared, she would. The thought of facing him after having acted so erratically was humiliating. He had probably laughed himself to sleep last night.

Swinging around she snapped the cold water on, snatched the coffee carafe and filled it with water. Busywork. That's what she needed to get her head on straight before she went in there and faced him. When she'd finished preparing the coffeemaker, she filled a glass with water, took another deep breath and reached for the pain medication.

She faltered when she saw the little white pill lying on the counter beside the bottle.

Exactly where she'd placed it last night.

She couldn't have? That poor man! She closed her eyes, willing herself to calm down.

It didn't work. Snatching up the pill and the glass of water, she hurried to Bob's room—and met him as he came around the corner.

She nearly tripped over her feet when she saw him. He was clutching his middle, supporting his ribs with one hand and gripping the door with the other hand.

How could she have forgotten to give him his pain killer!

"Good morning," he said. Despite the perspiration beaded across his forehead, he was smiling.

"Why didn't you call me?" she snapped. "I can not believe I left you stranded and didn't give you your medication. And what in the world are you doing up?" She was scolding him. The poor man was in a world of hurt and she was griping him out! "I am so sorry, here let me help you," she said, grasping what dignity she had left. She set the water and medicine on the table and moved to his side. Ignoring the silly grin on his lips, she slipped her arm around his waist.

"Molly, relax," he chuckled.

Chuckled!

"I don't normally take that heavy a painkiller anyway. I'm fine. I'm up."

"Barely," she snapped, and immediately felt like a toad. But he was chuckling. And in pain. And she was so frustrated. "I am so sorry," she managed. "For everything. C'mon. We'll get you to the couch and then you can take the medicine and feel better."

"Nope. Take me to the kitchen and the stool."

"But—"

"No buts. I'm not taking any more painkillers and I'm not getting back on that couch. I'm ready to start moving around a little."

They took a step together and she heard his sharp intake of air. "You need something."

"No, I don't. Kitchen, please." His eyes were crinkled around the edges, but he wasn't chuckling anymore and she knew it was taking everything he had to stand up.

His arm tightened around her shoulders and she nodded. "Okay, lean on me." They made slow progress, but they made it at last.

John Boy came scampering across the hardwood, lost his grip and slid into Bob's bare foot. They were almost to the bar stool. "Hey, little fella, I'd pet you but I can't bend over."

"He missed you terribly last night," she said, wanting to do something more for him. But what? She looked up at him and met his gaze straight on.

"You didn't get any sleep, did you?" he asked.

HOLD ME, COWBOY

Frozen and certain she was as pink as Lacy's hot pink salon, Molly shook her head. And despite everything, he smiled, letting those dimples play havoc with her mind.

Focus, Molly! Focus.

"Are you okay?" he asked.

She nodded her head, though nothing was okay.

"Fine," she managed. "Just lost my breath for a minute."

He leaned his head down so his lips were close to her ear. "Yeah, I know exactly what you mean."

CHAPTER TWELVE

Bob knew about calming skittish colts. He knew about calming skittish cattle. But he didn't know what to do for a skittish female.

Sitting at the kitchen island on a tall stool, he watched Molly prepare to change his bandages. Her fingers were shaking. He hadn't thought how upset forgetting to give him his medicine would make her.

"Molly, please relax. Believe it or not, sitting up high on this bar stool is a good thing. At least I can get myself up and down without hurting too much, so stop feeling guilty—especially if that's what's got you so worked up." He rubbed John Boy's back with the toe of his foot and smiled when the fat puppy rolled over, clawing at his toe with his paws. When Mr. Feisty suddenly took a bite of his toe, Bob yelped.

Molly's lips curved into a smile. "You have to watch

out for him." She tore open a package of fresh gauze and her shoulders relaxed.

"I'm learning as I go," he said, realizing it was true with both John Boy *and* Molly. He watched her walk toward him, and he almost smiled thinking about how she'd scolded him earlier. She was cute when she was frustrated.

"You know there is no way you can sit there all afternoon," she said. "The doctor said you need to take the pain medicine. You're going to have to get some sleep sometime. Rest helps a body heal." Her finely sculptured lips flattened into a straight line crinkling just a tinge at the edges and her eyes melted with concern.

She was back to herself and distractingly convincing with her argument.

"Molly, getting up from that bed was what had me hurting so bad earlier. I promise. But later, after I've moved around a little bit more, if I decide to get back on the couch to rest, I'll take some medicine, if that'll make you feel better."

"That'll make us both feel better," she said, peeling the paper away from the gauze and moving behind him. He could feel the warmth of her breath against his skin as she concentrated on changing his bandages. She smelled of fresh air and a warm sunlit morning. It was nice. It was habit-forming.

Now he was the one feeling skittish. He was treading in dangerous waters.

But he'd put his sane mind on later. Right now he was hurting too bad to force sanity into the mix. Despite his pain, he'd decided not to take any more painkillers.

Feeling her long, graceful fingers tending his bandages, he closed his eyes and let himself enjoy the moment. Her touch and the knowledge that she was in his home was all he needed at the moment. It was nice having someone take care of him. He'd realized last night while he lay awake thinking about her that the last thing he wanted to do while she was here was sleep. Yep, he was a messed-up cookie, because he didn't want to miss a single moment of Molly's company.

This attraction was a doomed state of affairs, but he'd think about that when the time came.

Now he just wanted to get to know her better. "So what would you like for breakfast?"

Her question surprised him. He glanced over his shoulder at her. She smiled then concentrated again on her task.

"I can cook some scrambled eggs. I'm not any good with fried ones, but scrambled I'm okay with. They're more forgiving."

"I thought you said you couldn't cook?"

She laughed, causing her fingers to tremble as she smoothed the bandage in place. Her laugh was a quiet sound, like a whisper that came out slightly too loud. He'd always admired it. Molly's laugh was one of those still, quiet sounds that lingered and made a guy want to do something in hopes of getting to hear it again. Yeah, he could listen to Molly laugh all day.

"I didn't say I couldn't cook. I said I couldn't cook well."

"Then throw some eggs in that skillet and let me see what you've got."

That got him another laugh. She pulled his shirt down then walked to the fridge. When she turned around, she held a carton of eggs and a jug of milk. "You eat breakfast at Sam's, don't you?"

"Every morning. Until lately." Now why had he said that? She paused and looked at him with troubled eyes.

"Sorry about that."

"Look, Molly, I didn't mean anything by that. Stop saying you're sorry. It's driving me mad."

The tension that had ebbed was back. "How can I not say I'm sorry? Look at you, Bob. You almost died out there and it's my fault. If you had been killed by that bull, it would have been totally my fault. Don't you see that? How can I not feel sorry?" She was looking at him with pleading eyes.

"Molly, do you want me to say I forgive you? Would that make you feel better? Because I do. I forgive you."

She blinked, then set the eggs on the counter and stood there in silent silhouette. He watched her blinking hard and thought it best not to say anything, to let her get control of her emotions. After a couple of minutes she sniffed, looked sideways at him with misted eyes. Big, beautiful, green eyes...sincere eyes.

"Thank you."

He nodded. He had to admit he could get used to having her in his home. In his life. He wondered what she thought about his home? Compared to hers. He wondered if she ever thought about buying a picture for her wall. If she ever thought about settling down.

He wondered why he was wondering.

* * *

"Do what?" Molly was standing at the sink rinsing out the coffee cups when she thought she heard him say he wanted to check on his cows. She spun around. "Check on your cows!" Molly was dumbfounded. They had shared a quick breakfast, talking about ranch life, something she knew very little about but was finding very interesting. "Bob, how are you going to check on your cows? Clint and Brady and the entire cowboy population of Mule Hollow are feeding your animals for you, so there is no need to worry about the cows. You said yourself that the truck ride here was tough."

He just laughed. "Molly—" He grimaced with pain. "That was not a good move. One thing about a man and his cows is it does a cowboy's heart good to see the hairy beasts every day. Don't ask me why, it's just a fact. I know there's no way I can tend them, but I can look at them. With your help that is."

Molly walked over and picked up the plates and carried them to the sink. How could she refuse an offer like that? She didn't see how it was going to happen, but if he thought he could do it then who was she to say no? Now she understood why he'd asked her earlier to help put his cowboy boot on.

"Okay. What do you want me to do?" She turned and caught him smiling at her. Her heart skipped a beat and she saw headlines—which she immediately backspaced over before she got the chance to read them.

"First, you can go and grab the set of binoculars off the desk in my office. I'd go get them myself, but it'd be tomorrow before we got to see the cows."

"Binoculars. This is sounding very interesting. You better go ahead and get started toward the back door. Me and the binoculars will catch up with you," she said drily, already heading to his office at the front of the house.

His laugh followed her out of the room and her stomach did a little dip—which she ignored. She had finally gotten hold of her senses and it was going to stay that way.

When she returned with the binoculars, he was standing beside the back door smiling as if he'd just climbed Mount Everest.

"Look at you! You made good time." She knew it had probably killed him getting to the door, but there were no beads of sweat on his brow, so that said something.

"I flew like the wind," he teased.

"Oh did you? What now?"

"Open the door and give me a lift, sweetheart."

"Okay, sugar baby," she said with a snort. The man was full of it. Opening the door, she slipped her arm around his waist again and waited as he carefully placed his good arm across her shoulders. His fingers brushed her cheek as he did so and their warmth sent a ripple of wonder through her.

Oh no, you don't, she thought, and promptly pushed the wondering away. Wondering would get a girl in trouble.

Bob reached the tree. He'd about killed himself doing it. His reasons for wanting to look at his cattle bothered him. He knew Clint was making certain his cattle were being well taken care of. Clint Matlock was the best cattleman around. So why was Bob nearly killing himself to get to the top of the ridge where he could catch a glimpse of a few of his herd?

Because it gave him an excuse to put his aching arm around Molly.

It wasn't as if he went around figuring out ways to put his arms around a woman. If truth be told, he hadn't actually held a woman in a very long time. He'd been too busy working and saving his money to buy this place. But that still didn't explain why he couldn't resist torturing himself by holding a woman close who had made no secret that she didn't want a family.

Looking down at the top of her chestnut head, he swallowed and took one more giant leap toward insanity by wondering what her hair felt like. It was thick.

Thick and shiny, and the rich color reminded him of the coat of a chestnut mare with the sunlight glinting off it. And it smelled like flowers. Not like the overpowering scents on the envelopes in his dining room, but more like an essence of flowers. Just enough to make him want to lean down and inhale a little deeper. They'd made it to the tree in time to save him from making a complete fool of himself. Shaken by the ideas churning in his ailing brain, he quickly grabbed the low limb for support and willed her to move as far away from him as possible. Which she did quicker than he'd expected, almost as if she could read his mind. She didn't just move away, it was more like she ran.

She took five quick steps, hugged her right arm around her middle and toyed with the chain at her neck with the other.

She didn't look at him, which was a good thing. Right. Then why was he watching her, waiting to catch her gaze sliding to his? Hoping to see some glimmer of the same infatuation for him that he found himself feeling for her?

It didn't happen. Like a statue she stood, back ramrod stiff, and watched his cattle in the distance. He, on the other hand, knew what they looked like.

"So there they are," she said, letting go of her charm to wave a graceful hand toward the animals.

HOLD ME, COWBOY

"There they are." He continued to study her.

She turned toward him and caught him. She tilted her head slightly and crossed a long jean-clad leg at the ankles. It made her appear even more lanky than she was.

His stomach clenched and he took a deep breath and tried to picture her in Europe somewhere, with a pencil tucked behind her ear as she interviewed some war-ravaged—he couldn't even think the words much less picture it. She was too young. Too fragile. Too... he couldn't think about it. Nothing about the situation seemed right to him.

"I saw the pictures in your office of you as a bullfighter. It amazed me. That one where the photographer caught you doing a somersault in the air over the bull—I guess he'd thrown you?"

"Yeah. I was actually taking the hit for the bull rider and it sent me flying." He was glad to have something to talk about. Less thinking time.

"Did that one hurt you?"

"Not that one."

"And that other one, the one where you were diving across the bull's back? That photo was remarkable."

"The rider was hung up. I was trying to get at the rope to free his hand."

"You took a lot of chances."

He shrugged and then wished he hadn't when the pain shot through him. "I was quick, well trained. It was a calculated risk."

She frowned. "Hey, buddy. You're talking to a reporter. I do my homework on my subject matter. I saw the articles. The injury rate. The deaths."

"Absent from the body, present with the Lord. Every job has its dangers. And I have an insurance policy that's a one-way ticket to heaven. So what's there to be afraid of?"

She smiled. "True. So then why did you quit?"

He leaned against the old oak tree and studied the distance. "It was time."

"How did you know?" She tilted her head and the crease between her eyebrows deepened. "Really. What caused you to know?"

He studied her inquisitive expression. "You're just full of questions. Is all of this off-the-record?"

She blushed again. "Everything about you is officially classified information from this moment on." She held up her right hand and smiled solemnly.

He leaned carefully against the tree, taking some more weight off his bad leg. "There were several things, actually. First, I'd always dreamed of having a family, but I had too much junk inside me to think it was something I could ever really have. I was an angry kid."

Her eyes widened in disbelief. "Really? I would never in a million years have pictured you as angry. I mean, other than getting angry at what I did to you, you've always been so cool and collected. How old were you?"

She appeared keenly interested in what he had to say. It was obvious why people opened up to her. "Nineteen when I started. I actually started out on a bull."

"Riding a bull?"

"Don't look so horrified. I never got hurt on top of a bull. Anyway, I was sitting on the fence after my ride, watching a buddy, and his hand got hung up. He was being dragged and tossed around like a dishrag and the bullfighters weren't having any luck getting his hand loose. I was afraid for him, so I jumped into the fray, grabbed onto the rope and freed him. It felt natural, and after that I never went back on a bull. I realized I liked staring the bull down from the ground. Saving lives can be addictive."

"And second?"

Always the reporter, she guided him back for the rest of the story. "I met the Lord. And surrendered my life to Him and suddenly I started thinking about settling down. About the family I'd dreamed of as a kid. There are some great Christian bullfighters out there, with families and the whole big witness for the Lord going on. But bullfighters are on the road constantly. I wanted a family and a life with them. Not just a life supporting them." He paused to look around his ranch. "And I wanted this. I still have a lot to do, but it's coming together."

She smiled and moved closer. "How did you end up in Mule Hollow?"

He grinned at her. "I was on my way to the finals in Las Vegas and had a flat just outside of Mule Hollow. I'd traveled that road four years in a row and that year I decided to take a shortcut. Don't know why I did it, but I did, and for the first time ever I had a flat tire. I was just finishing up putting on the spare when Clint stopped to see if I needed a hand. We got to talking, ended up driving to Sam's for lunch and before I left, he offered me a job if I ever got tired of bullfighting." He and Clint had clicked immediately. "I thought about his offer and about Mule Hollow all the way to Vegas. I couldn't get it out of my head. I'd been looking for the Lord to lead me to the right place and I liked the wide-open spaces and the people, few that there were." He smiled. "When I got to Vegas, all through the event I had to force myself to focus. That's not a good thing when you have people depending on you. You earn the opportunity to be a bullfighter at the Pro Bull Rider's finals. The top bull riders in the association have to vote you in. They have to say they're willing to trust their lives to the bullfighters they vote for. It's an honor that I didn't take lightly. If I couldn't focus solely on their safety, it was time to move on.

When the three days were over, I packed up my gear and came back to Mule Hollow."

She was studying him. "When did you move your things here?"

He looked at the ground then lifted his head to smile at her. "Everything I owned was in the camper of my truck. When I was in between events I stayed with buddies. I was ready to settle down." He knew what it was like to own nothing because you were just passing through.

"That quick?" She said the words as if they were a mystery.

"Yeah, that quick."

Bob was sleeping. Molly stood over him, relieved to see the tension relaxed from his face as he rested. By the time they'd made the walk back to the house, Bob had been in a world of pain. His shortness of breath and the drawn look in his eyes couldn't be hidden from her. She had to practically shove the medicine down his throat in order to get him to take it. But once he'd realized she wasn't backing down, he'd given in. That alone spoke volumes for the way he was feeling. But the man acted as if he didn't want to go to sleep.

She'd helped him settle into the recliner. They'd decided it might ease the transition from sitting to lying down, which, as Bob had described the feeling, was a fate worse than death. Thankfully the recliner worked well.

Very gently she spread the soft blanket over him and again couldn't resist lightly brushing a dark curl off his forehead. The man was brave, powerful and dear. Some woman was going to be so lucky—no, the word was *blessed*. Some lucky woman was going to be so *blessed* to become Mrs. Bob Jacobs. From a distance she'd believed he would be the perfect husband. Now she knew it firsthand. She wanted him to have the life he wanted. He deserved it.

Her heart suddenly ached and she turned away, walking back to the kitchen. She pulled her laptop from her backpack and sat at the kitchen table only to find herself analyzing his home once more instead of writing.

Home was so important to him. It was enough to make a girl want to settle down and join in on the dream.

Whoa! Back up there, Molly girl.

That thought sent her racing outside to a chair on the porch. She had a column to turn in and an article to wrap up—the distractions of Bob's home were not going to let her take care of business. Her mind set, she settled into a patio chair and focused on her work, not her increasing inner turmoil.

An hour later, she finished and reread her work. It was a little different. It had a different tone from her other work, but she liked it. She liked it a lot. Instead of the lighter, airy voice she normally used for her Mule Hollow pieces, today there was a bit more introspection in her work. She had started the article exploring the reasons behind significant life-changing decisions. Namely, people reaching the crossroads in their lives when they decide the time has come to settle down. And even though the article made no mention of Mule Hollow or Bob, they had both planted the seed. Bob's sudden and definitive decision to instantly change his life intrigued her. Plus, she'd originally been drawn to Mule Hollow because Lacy had moved here so quickly and decisively. Molly scanned the article, convinced people would be as interested as she was. She just needed to add in statistics on the percentage of people who changed their lives on whims. Then she would tweak it a bit and send it out. She knew immediately which magazine she would target first.

Making a living as a freelance writer was like juggling. In order to sell, she constantly kept numerous articles in circulation at all times. Not all would get picked up by magazines or periodicals, but she was developing relationships with several editors and gaining a feel for just the slant an article needed to fit each one. She made a decent wage and she sometimes wondered why she dreamed of writing grittier, more journalistic fare when the strong point of her work was the down-home charm she brought to the plate. She was very good at what she did. But was she good enough to make it in the world outside the safe boundaries of rural America?

And did she really want to? Had she dreamed a little dream as a frightened kid and that was merely all it was to be? All she truly wanted it to be?

Less than a week ago she'd not allowed herself to entertain this question. It had seemed that doing so was a sign she was giving up on her dream. And she would fight tooth and nail to hang on to that dream.

But suddenly it was a question she couldn't seem to stop thinking about.

She lowered her head and prayed for discernment. As a fairly new Christian, she was learning that God gave freely of Himself, but had she been asking the right questions?

CHAPTER THIRTEEN

The following morning, Molly arrived at Bob's to find him standing on the porch deep in discussion with Clint.

"Hey, Molly, how's it going?" Clint asked as she carried John Boy up the gravel path.

"Bob," she scolded. "What are you doing?" He looked as if he hadn't slept at all. "You are pushing yourself too hard."

He frowned. "Good morning to you, too, Sunshine." She knit her eyebrows together and glared at him.

"Clint, he acts like he's not all broken up inside."

Clint pushed the rim of his hat up with his thumb and laughed. "Most cowboys have had a broken rib at some point. That's part of the business. Hazard of the job. If we didn't fight being down, we'd be in the wrong profession."

HOLD ME, COWBOY

Bob lifted an eyebrow at her. "See."

Molly shook her head. They were like boys.

Clint looked from her to Bob. "Well, I'll get going. I'll check with you when I get back up to the barn, Bob."

"Is something wrong?" She looked from Clint to Bob.

"Yesterday Clint noticed a couple a babies that weren't nursing like they need to be so he's about to go round them up and bring them to the pens by the barn so we can bottle-feed them."

"Is there anything I can do to help?" Molly had been itching to get in a little ranch experience. Experience was the spice of a reporter's words.

"Have you ever bottle fed?" Clint asked.

"Nope. But it can't be that hard."

Bob grinned and Clint laughed hard.

"You sound like Lacy," Clint said, his good-looking face lighting up at the mention of Lacy. "She didn't think it would be difficult either until she did it."

Did they think she couldn't care for a calf? "Lacy bottle-fed a calf?"

His expression softened. "Oh, yeah, after a bit. Now she treats those cows like kids. If they weren't so big she'd load them up in that pink monstrosity of hers and take them on one of her beloved joyrides."

Lacy loved joyriding in her pink convertible. She was the most spontaneous, life-loving, God-loving person Molly had ever met. She inspired Molly to let go and try new things, like feeding calves. Molly lifted her chin and squared her shoulders. "Could I try feeding them?" She looked at Bob then back to Clint. "I mean, Bob can't, and you have plenty of other more important things to do. Right?"

He studied her for a moment. "That's up to Bob. I'll be back."

"Well, what do you think?" she asked, not liking the skepticism in Bob's eyes.

"They can get pushy and obstinate."

"So, are you telling me not to attempt it?"

"No, of course you can do it. I just don't want you taking on more than you can handle. Molly, I already hate the thought of you putting your life on hold for me. I don't want you having to tend to my other problems, too."

She plopped a hand to her hip. So that was it. "I thought we talked about this. I got you into this and I'm going to get you out of it. And if that includes taking care of some of your livestock then so be it. Besides, I want to find out what is so intriguing about the cowboy way of life. I want some hands-on experience. This will be fun!" Cowboys loved their jobs. It seemed they enjoyed going to work even though the work was long and hard. She was intrigued by that. She wanted to experience the why of it all. It would enhance her articles.

"All right," he said. "If you'll help me put on my boot, I'll help you get the gear together and instruct you on how it's done."

"I'm sure Clint can show me. The barn is farther away than the tree was yesterday. There's no need for you to push yourself that hard."

"Molly. Stop. I'm not a baby, and no matter how much you try, I am not sitting around the house all day. If I've got calves that need attention, I'm going to at least check on them. Besides, I can't let you have all the fun now, can I?"

It was like arguing with a fence post. "Fine," she snapped. "But you have to at least take some aspirin." He was a stubborn man. She was just starting to realize how much. If he wanted to hurt himself then she couldn't stop him. She wasn't his mother. She wondered about his mother. About his past. About why he'd been an angry teenager.

"Wait here," she said. She stalked into the kitchen and yanked a bottle of over-the-counter pain medicine from the cabinet. She doubted that it would do any more than take the edge off his pain, but at least it would be something.

The man needed a keeper.

Problem was, she'd been his keeper for all of three days now and she was realizing that she liked the job way too much!

"Molly, you can't be afraid of him if you want to catch him."

Molly stood in the center of the stall, staring at the sleek black calf with the huge droopy ears. She had seen cattle out in the pastures, but hadn't ever really paid a lot of attention to anything different about the Brahman breed except that they did have those huge humps on their backs. Now, standing in the pen staring at the good-size baby cow, she was realizing that with their floppy ears they looked like gigantic hound dogs. The baby standing in front of her was not a hound dog though. He was actually a deceptive little con artist.

And far, far from the tiny baby she'd expected. He had to weigh a hundred pounds, maybe two. Not a newborn as she'd been expecting. Looking at him, she felt like a city gal on the reality TV series *Cowboy U*. He blinked at her and gave her an *I'm just a little baby* look. Oh sure, a con artist was exactly what he was, standing there pretending to be all shy and docile with

HOLD ME, COWBOY

his dreamy black eyes and his velvety nose when in fact she knew the truth.

Docile, ha! After two embarrassing failed attempts at catching him, and one sore backside, she knew the hard truth. Despite the calm way he batted his big eyelids at her, he'd evaded capture with the ease of a greased pig! A big pig.

This was a kink in her offer she hadn't thought about. "I guess I figured the little darlings were going to just come up and take the bottle from me. Imagine that. What a dunce I was. Just like I thought they were going to be about fifty pounds, too."

"If it didn't hurt so much, I'd laugh at that one."

Molly shot him a glare. He'd been standing there on the outside of the fence calmly giving her directions as if he was choreographing a ballet or something. He had the patience of Job, but sadly she had no talent. Maybe she couldn't do this.

She straightened her shirt, pushed her hair out of her face, sucked in her gut and stared down at the calf. She had not been beaten. Oh, no. She'd tried cooing sweetly to him—that had got her slammed into the gate as he kicked and bucked away from her. She'd tried begging—that had got her pretty much the same response and a "please don't beg my cows" groan from Bob.

So now she was trying the firm, calm approach. "There, that's better, Molly. You can do this. Just be more aggressive and I promise you before the night is over you will have fed both calves. Now show him who the boss is. Get dirty if you have to."

"I am dirty. Didn't you see me hit the dirt in that first fiasco?"

"Yeah, I saw it. Now that you aren't worried about it anymore, you'll get him. Pretend you're Clint Eastwood."

"What?" Molly glared at him again.

"Yeah, that's it, Dirty Harry. Now walk him into that corner and grab him around the neck."

Molly's mouth dropped. "Are you telling me I look like Clint Eastwood? I mean, really, he's a good-looking man, but I don't think you're getting Brownie points right now, buster."

Bob did laugh at that and then groaned, and Molly cringed, seeing the pain on his face. But really, you didn't tell a girl she looked like Dirty Harry.

"Molly," he said, taking a deep breath. "All I'm saying is get more of that 'Do you feel lucky?' kind of attitude and go for it. Believe me, on your worst day times a hundred, you could not look like a man."

Molly pushed back her shoulders at the compliment and smiled apologetically. "Oh." Now that sounded more like it. Taking a deep breath, she spread her feet shoulder width apart, shook her hands and rolled her shoulders to loosen them up. Then she gave the calf a glare. "So tell me," she said as he blinked at her and flopped one foot-size ear so that it slapped the side of his neck. It was obvious he couldn't care less about anything she had to say. But she said it anyway. "Do you feel lucky? Or are you going to make my day?"

He lowered his sleek head, and his ears almost touched the soft dirt as Molly made her move. Having learned from her earlier mistakes, she faked right then dove left just as he bolted straight into her waiting arms! With a whoop she snagged him around the neck as Bob had instructed her earlier and held on with every tired fiber of her being. But he refused to give in easily. "Oh, no you're not. Don't you know I just want to feed you?" She dug her heels in and skittered across the soft dirt, her right arm locked around his neck. Her teeth and her brain rattled in her head like gravel on spin cycle, but she hung on.

"You've got him. Don't let go," Bob yelled.

She had him! And then he put on the brakes, did a Houdini and she flipped like a pancake and splatted face first in the soft dirt.

"Molly. You okay?"

Coughing, she lay still, berating herself for once

more letting the baby get the best of her.

"Molly?"

She gritted her teeth, regretting it immediately when she chewed the dirt. "I'm okay. You win. This cowboy thing is not as easy as it looks."

"You're doing fair. Really. You should have seen me at my first calf scramble. I was hot, tired and as filthy as you are."

She looked up and crawled to her knees. "Is that so?"

"Yup. But I got one in the end. You just can't give up."

"Am I going to have to do this every time I try to feed them?" Although she'd been warned, she could only take so much abuse.

"Believe it or not after a couple of times, they're going to love you like their mother. You'll be like 'Mary Had a Little Lamb.' You'll just have two huge Brahman bulls following behind you."

"Wonderful." She pictured these two young bulls as adults, massive walls of muscle, their powerful shoulders and the huge signature hump on their backs tagging along behind her. And their long ears, which seemed at odds with such an intimidating animal, flopping in the wind. "I can't picture that," she said, grunting as she stood up. She could, however, imagine what she looked like. Pigpen from the *Peanuts* clan came to mind. So much for being thrilled that Bob thought she was cute. She spit out the dirt in her mouth, which she was certain made her all the more appealing. Especially when she had to do it a second time.

Slick was standing there batting his eyes at her again and they were actually close to the corner, which gave her hope. Bob had been saying to keep him in the corner. With a valiant effort Molly dove—and caught him! One more time.

"There you go. Now throw a leg over him."

"A leg? What do you mean, a leg?"

"You have to throw a leg over him, wrap your left arm under his neck to hold him in place and then when I hand you the bottle you have to force him to take it."

"What do you mean, force it? He won't just take it?"

"Sorry. That's just the way it is. After a while they learn."

"Yeah, but what about in the meantime?" She was hanging on to him, in the corner with every muscle in her body. Grunting with effort, she threw her leg over his back, planted her feet and locked his shoulders with her thighs as he bucked.

"Oh no, you don't," she growled. Just like Bob had instructed, she slid her arm around his neck, maneuvered her elbow under his chin, and suddenly she actually felt some control. Oh, my goodness. She finally had the upper hand!

"Here's the bottle."

Glancing up, she took the offered bottle. It was about the size of a two-quart pitcher and the red bottle nipple was huge. Taking it in her hand she pushed it toward the calf's mouth. He tried to spit it away, but Molly hadn't come this far to take no for an answer.

"Come on, sweetie, I know you're just a scared baby and I want to take care of you." She wasn't certain if it was the gentle urgings or the prayer she was praying, but after a couple of tries he started smacking away at the formula. "Look, he's doing it!" she exclaimed, sporting a grin so big it felt like it was coming up from her toes. She'd never been so grateful in all her life. Or so rewarded.

Or so slimed!

Laughing, she struggled to maintain a grip on the large bottle as the baby got greedy—smacking and tugging and slobbering all over the place.

She could hear Bob on the other side of the fence fighting laughter and she glanced over at him. His eyes were sparkling and his dimples were showing despite the pain on his face from the mixture of laughter and broken ribs.

She knew she was filthy, but it didn't matter. She had never felt so satisfied in all of her life.

He'd said the cowboy life could be addictive. Looking at him, she knew it was true, especially with Bob working beside her.

A bawling cry drew her attention and as she turned her head she was greeted by a big wet nose when curious Baby Two stepped up beside her.

"I think the second one might be a little easier on you," Bob said, a smile in his voice. "He knows something good is going on for his buddy. Are you up for it?"

Molly looked from Bob to the calf, which was nudging the arm that held the bottle for the first calf, and she smiled. She'd almost forgotten she had another calf to go. "Oh, yeah. I'm in all right," she laughed. If she hadn't been afraid of scaring the babies she'd have hollered a good ol' Texas yee-haw! Which was something totally out of character for her.

And she liked that.

She liked it very much, actually.

CHAPTER FOURTEEN

She was killing him. Whoever said laughter was the best medicine obviously didn't have broken ribs. Watching Molly wrestle the calves down in an attempt to force-feed them was a riot. Any other time he'd have enjoyed watching a greenhorn get her first taste of dirt. But this was torture. Entertaining as all get out, but torture nonetheless.

She'd been knocked down, dragged around, bucked off and almost kicked—which had caused him to start to bolt to help her, an action that was almost impossible. Through it all, Molly hadn't given up. He'd come to realize tenacity was Molly's secret weapon. He admired her for it.

Watching her now, as she eased off the back of the baby Brahman, empty bottle in her hand, her eyes were gleaming. Bob couldn't take his eyes from her as she walked toward him, filthy, completely worn-out, smiling.

Now that was a woman he could love.

* * *

"So how do you feel?" Bob asked from his perch on the bar stool the following morning. He was tapping information into his laptop computer with his two index fingers.

Molly groaned and limped toward the coffee machine. "Whoa, baby! I have never enjoyed a day more but what a horrible way to wake up. I never knew I had that many muscles." She smiled, looking beat. "We make a pair now, don't we?"

"Like twins," he laughed, but caught it before it was hard enough to hurt his ribs. Molly was moving slower than him this morning and he was anxious to see how she was going to catch Baby One and Baby Two moving like that. She paused, pouring her coffee, and pinned her grass green eyes on him.

"Look at you," she drawled, letting out a low whistle. "You look like you're feeling much better than yesterday."

Her appreciative gaze prodded him to sit up straighter and force his stitched shoulders back a bit more. "I actually got some sleep last night." He wanted her to keep looking at him like that. "The ribs are still killing me, but look." He lifted his good arm above his head. "See, full range of motion." The stitched shoulder was still tight, but he only had three more days before the stitches came out and he'd be on the road to working again. And time spent with Molly would be over. The thought took the joy right out of the moment as he watched her amble toward him. "Just don't make me laugh."

"Hey, I can't promise anything. That's up to your babies. They're the ones that made a clown out of me," she said, then winked at him.

Bob's heart sucker-punched his broken ribs from the inside and it was all he could do not to gasp.

"Honestly, Bob, I had such a good time yesterday. Painful, but *really* fun. I think moving around will help me the way it helped you."

Her smile was like dawn breaking through the morning fog. His tongue stuck to the roof of his mouth and he suddenly had the oddest feeling he'd kissed her before. Okay, enough about the kissing. "Remember, I told you bullfighting was addictive. Well, so is ranching."

It occurred to him that maybe he simply had an addictive personality, because he was finding the more he was around Molly, the less he wanted to be away from her. He'd done nothing but think of her every second after she'd left him the night before. For the longest moment they stared at each other. All he had to do was lean down slightly and he would know what it felt like to really kiss Molly, not just imagine it.

In the distance the bawl of a calf pierced the moment. It brought reality back into play and him to his senses.

"C'mon, I've got the bottles ready." He spun toward the counter by the door, paying for it when his ribs ground together in open rebellion. He grimaced as he picked up the two bottles he'd prepared earlier with the special milk replacement formula appropriate for the size and weight of each calf. Despite his misgivings about what he was feeling around Molly, he was glad to be moving a little livelier. It was a macho thing, he knew, but he could feel Molly's eyes on him and frankly he was tired of being crippled around her.

"You *are* feeling better."

He stood straighter, holding the door for her with his good arm, then rubbed his jaw. "I even managed to shave this morning so I'm a human again. Sleeping in the chair is a great help. Thanks for thinking of it. One night of getting up and down on that bed was enough to make me grateful to have a chair to sleep in. The only drawback to not being so decrepit is I don't get to wrap my arm around a pretty girl."

Molly shot him a startled look. "If you say so," she said, groaning as she bent to rub John Boy's head when he yelped for attention from his pen at the side of the porch. "I guess we better leave him here again so he doesn't get stomped by Baby One or Two."

"For now. But he's a cow dog, so part of his learning experience will be understanding how to be around the cattle." He eased down the steps, glad Molly had turned her back to him. He'd squelched a grunt, but he was certain she'd have seen its mark on his expression. Once down, he stopped to catch his wind and to let the screaming of his insides calm down. Of course he tried to tell himself he was only waiting for Molly to catch up. He was startled when she reached for the bottles. "Put your arm over my shoulders," she demanded.

"I heard your steps falter, and don't think for one moment I believe you are telling me the entire truth about not hurting."

He wasn't going to argue, not when she smelled as good as she did and already had her arm around his waist. Bending his head close to her ear, he whispered, "I think you just missed my arms around you."

She laughed. "You wish. Truth is, we can help each

other."

He chuckled and held her tighter. He knew she would be leaving. She wasn't anyone he needed to be having thoughts about, because she didn't fit into any of his parameters for the wife he was looking for. But he enjoyed her company. He always had. From the first day they'd met, they'd clicked.

How many times since she'd moved to Mule Hollow had his mind wandered to thoughts of her? Last night he'd continually thought of the time they'd spent together at the very first revive-the-town Fair Day just after the women had hatched their Wives Needed campaign. He'd been roped into working the lemonade booth by Adela and there had been a swarm of women lined up to buy Adela's unbelievable lemonade. He would never forget turning around with a glass in his hand and coming face-to-face with Molly. She'd taken his breath away.

Okay, enough of that, cowboy. He'd do well to remind himself that she was just passing time in Mule Hollow until something better came along.

Eyeing the barn, which was still a good twenty-five yards away, he went where he didn't want to go. "So how's it going with your career?"

"Well, great actually. Mule Hollow has given me more of a boost career-wise than I could ever have imagined. I mean, I'd thought when I started the column that I had something unique. But I never dreamed that you cowboys would get this much press. I'm—" she blushed "—I'm actually a big hit."

He knew about that. His dad had become an overnight success with the recognition of one story. He forced himself not to focus on that. Molly was different. She didn't have ties. She didn't have a family to forget about. It wasn't fair to put her into the same category as his dad.

"I'm glad for you," he said, instead. "You've worked hard for this."

His heart seemed to falter when she looked up at him and her hand on his waist tightened slightly.

"Thank you," she said. "I've wanted this all my life. I really think I have a shot at landing this contributing editor position with *World View* magazine. It's a step up and means some travel abroad."

Her expression bloomed and he wondered how it would feel to have her look at him like that.

"Which I've always wanted to do," she continued, totally oblivious to his wondering mind.

He was familiar with the magazine and, grudgingly, he had to admit that Molly's work was a perfect fit. "When will you know something?"

She looked up at him and he looked away. "Soon,

I think."

They walked a few more steps in silence. He struggled to be happy for her but found it hard.

"I didn't mean for it to sound like I was just in it for the travel," she said. "It's about the places and reasons for the travel. You know, my stories. This will give me a chance to stretch my wings. I know I can do some good out there."

He wanted to say that she was doing good here, in Mule Hollow, but wouldn't that be hypocritical of him after the way he'd reacted to her articles?

Truth was, she *was* making a difference, but he didn't say so.

Molly was feeling pretty good about the whole experience. It was the evening of her fourth day with Bob and she'd once again fed the two obstinate calves. Bob said the two bad boys had been with their mamas too long on the range and that was the reason they were so ornery and didn't know how to treat a lady. But despite their bad manners, she relished the challenge and had come out the victor once again as they'd both finished their bottles and eaten some dry grain Bob had brought them.

"How cool was that?" she asked herself, standing

there watching her boys eat. "Outstanding. That's what it was. Absolutely outstanding."

There was something to be said for taking care of animals. And to have Bob's glowing approval made it that much better. They had shared a nice day—feeding the boys that morning then relaxing with John Boy on the back porch until the boys' second feeding time rolled around. There were times, though, she felt something was bothering Bob. It had taken a lot of skill on her part to get him to finally open up to her and talk about his dreams for the run down ranch he'd bought.

But when he'd finally started talking about it, it had touched her heart. He was as focused on his life goals as she was on hers.

They were a lot alike, she realized, at least on goal-setting. Their life goals couldn't be any more different. His goal—to be a family man. Her goal…well, her goal didn't include a family. But as she sat listening to him talk, her heart warmed to his vision of his future. This beautiful land he'd bought with its rolling hills and lush grasses would someday soon be home to a cattle ranch of substance similar to the one Clint Matlock ran, as Bob had explained, only on a smaller scale. It would support a family, and for Bob that was all that mattered. A strong sense of longing enveloped Molly. She pushed it away. She'd been here for a couple days shy of a week and understood that her days were numbered. Despite everything that had happened since she'd spent time in Bob's world, nothing had changed. She didn't fit here.

"I think your hard work deserves a reward," Bob said, breaking into her thoughts as she came out of the pen, the second feeding behind her.

They started walking slowly back up to the house. His arm was draped across her shoulders and she could tell every step was an effort. She could relate, but she was not complaining in the least. "Oh, really. And what would that reward be?"

"Dinner at Sam's."

She glanced up at him. "You're too tired for that. And besides, riding in the car or truck would hurt too much."

"Hey," he said, giving her that playful grin.

She lifted an eyebrow. "Hay is for cows," she said, unable not to react to his good humor.

He squeezed her affectionately with his arm. "Aren't you Miss Smarty-Pants! I can make it, if you can drive. You deserve not to cook, and I'd like to see everyone. And in case you forgot, tonight Sam's is starting Thursday night all-you-can-eat catfish."

Molly gasped. "How could I have forgotten that?" She stopped at the porch. "And I thought you were just trying to stop me messing up your kitchen again."

"So what do you say?"

"If you're up for it, I am. I'd honestly hate to miss it." It didn't take long for them to wash their hands and faces, dust off their clothes and head toward town. Since Mule Hollow was a small cattle town, dusty diners were welcome at Sam's. Because of this, Molly wasn't too self-conscious about her appearance. After all, she was living authentically as a cowboy for the time being. She had successfully fed baby bulls, which entitled her to wear her dirt proudly.

She eased the truck over the cattle guard, trying to keep Bob as comfortable as possible. He gave no indication that he was in pain. She knew he was, but she was getting used to the idea that he didn't allow himself to pander to it.

"My mailbox is gone."

"What?" Molly asked more in surprise than actually as a question. Sure enough, the post that his mailbox had been fastened to was bare.

"Who would steal your mailbox?"

"No telling. I'll mention it to Brady. Chalk it up to one more bizarre happening in my life this week." Molly cringed inwardly. She'd almost forgotten that the reason she was spending time with Bob was because of the trouble she'd caused in his life.

HOLD ME, COWBOY

He covered her hand on the steering wheel. "Don't let that statement make you start feeling bad again."

She glanced at him and found sincerity in his eyes. "I mean it, Molly. I've enjoyed these last few days and don't regret a minute of anything that made time spent with you possible."

Molly thought that was the sweetest thing anyone had ever said to her. Especially after what she'd put him through. But that was just the kind of thing that made Bob, *Bob*.

The rest of the way into town she wondered about the mailbox. Whoever had stolen it had actually given Bob a blessing in disguise. At least for a little while there was nothing to advertise, at the nondescript cattle guard, who lived over the hill. Though the newspaper only sent the mail general delivery and hadn't given out his address, it was still easy enough for anyone who wanted directions to get them when they arrived in town. The missing mailbox would make finding Bob a little harder for his crazed fans.

The diner was packed when they walked in. Cassie greeted them with a squeal and open arms. She'd begun working some mornings and evenings for Sam since he'd started staying open later, a fact that, in itself, reflected the town's growth.

"Bob, you're out!" she exclaimed after her

initial squeal had alerted everyone to his presence. She gently hugged him and Molly had to smile watching her. Though she'd come to town targeting Bob for marriage, his compassion for the girl had helped her through a tough time and solidified a big brother–little sister friendship between them.

The small diamond solitaire on Cassie's left ring finger caught Molly's attention. "What is this?" she asked, taking Cassie's hand when she let go of Bob. Of course, she knew from the glow on her young face what it was.

"Jake popped the question," she gushed, moving her hand so that the small diamond caught the light and sparkled. "Isn't it the absolute most beautiful ring you have ever seen?"

Bob leaned in, looking at it then her, his expression intense. "I'm assuming Brady has spoken with Jake and laid down the law to him." Bob's voice was stern. It drew a laugh from Cassie and made Molly's insides go all gushy. The man was too cute.

"Yes, he did," Cassie replied, wonder in her words. "You'd think he was my daddy the way he scared poor Jake to death with all that serious talk about how he has to cherish me and take care of me."

Molly was touched once again by the sweetness of God's love and the way He'd protected Cassie. She also said a prayer of thanksgiving that her articles had been used to lead Cassie to Mule Hollow. She never knew exactly how God was going to use what she put on paper, but it was reassuring to know that He was in control. It gave Molly more confidence that maybe God would use this mess she'd made of Bob's life for good. Maybe his wife really was in those letters. She decided that tomorrow she'd start sorting through them again. If Mrs. Bob Jacobs was in that pile, Molly was determined to sort her out and do a little matchmaking of her own.

Cassie smiled. "Well, I've got to get back to work. If the two of you will visit for a few minutes, I'll have your table cleared off in a second. Sam's busy at the fryer, and even though he's got Hank Wilcox and Roy Don Jenkins back there helping him, they're having a hard time keeping up with the cooking. That leaves me to wait the tables and clear by myself."

"I can help you if you need me to," Molly offered, but Cassie shook her head.

"No way, this is my gig. Believe me, this ain't nothing compared to when I waited tables in Austin. Just give me a minute."

Molly's and Bob's eyes connected as Cassie hurried away. "One thing you don't do with that girl is step into her territory."

Bob nodded. "I think it's from growing up in the system. She had to be assertive to survive."

Molly smiled at him with admiration. "It's nice that you're her friend."

He placed his hand at the base of her back, giving her a gentle push toward the crowd of people. "I'm a better person for having met her. Thank you for bringing her into my life."

Molly looked up at him over her shoulder.

"Close your mouth, Molly. That's right. If it wasn't for you, she wouldn't be here. Safe and in love. You did a good thing with those articles. And if it took me getting stalked a little bit, then like I told you earlier, it was worth it."

Molly wasn't sure why that statement made her sad but it did. She blinked and then was saved by the crowd as they engulfed them. Dinner at Sam's had always felt more like what Molly figured a family reunion would feel like. People clustered together talking and laughing with one another, passing out hugs and slaps on the back as they told stories and shared their day.

Walking through the group, feeling Bob's touch on her back, Molly experienced a connection she'd never felt before.

CHAPTER FIFTEEN

The calves were hollering for breakfast as soon as they reached the gate the next morning. Molly didn't waste any time. She strode into the pen, talking calmly, and was shocked when Baby Two came up to her and all but asked for his morning bottle.

"Look at him, Bob! Baby Two knows me. He actually wants me to feed him."

"I told you it would get easier. I'll be calling you Mary pretty soon."

Reminded of what he'd said the first day, she laughed and happily started humming "Mary Had a Little Lamb" as Baby Two greedily sucked his formula down. He bumped her with his flat head a couple of times and Bob explained it was natural for them to bump their mamas while they nursed.

She couldn't explain how happy that made her. Just

think, she was the mother of a hairy, humpbacked, hundred-pound baby boy! Wonders never seemed to cease out here in the country.

Of course Baby One, always the wise guy, promptly dragged her around the pen like a dishrag and left her lying in the dirt as if he'd never seen her before in his life!

Bob was hurting, his insides shaking with laughter as he watched Baby One bring Molly straight off her mountaintop by sending her to the dirt once again. Breathing heavy, Molly propped up on her elbows and glared first at him then Baby One. "So you think this is funny, do you?"

"Hey, I told you not to make me laugh." His ribs were killing him, but he couldn't help chuckling at the picture she made. "I'm telling you, honey, just when you think you have these kids figured out they change course on you. Parenthood—who says you need to travel the world to find adventure?"

She shook her head, huffing out a stream of breath. "I don't have a comeback to that at the moment. I have to say this *has* been an interesting, though dirty, adventure. But I'm not so sure I'll be able to walk tomorrow."

"Well, rest easy. I'll repay the favor and be glad to take care of you if I need to."

Spitting dirt, Molly rolled to her knees and pushed up from the ground, grunting. She made a cute picture in her jeans, which accented the length of her legs, and her lavender shirt. Dirty or not, he could watch her maneuver around in the pen all day.

"Third time's the charm," she said, latching on to the runaway calf.

And it was. He dragged her when she grabbed him, but she found her feet, and manhandled him into the corner. Then holding on to him like a pro, she extended her hand for the bottle, not looking at him but instead concentrating on talking sweetly to Baby One. Bob passed the bottle through the fence, overwhelmingly proud of the effort she'd put out. When his fingers touched hers, he had to fight the urge to hang on.

There was no denying it. Every moment that passed made it harder for him to pretend he didn't care.

"We made progress with Baby Two, so there's still hope for One," she said, taking the bottle and breaking contact with him, completely unaware that he was fighting a battle he'd just realized he couldn't win.

Struggling to push away the morose reality smothering him, he focused on being in the moment. "If they'd been newborns, it wouldn't have been so strenuous. But since they're older and stronger and you're a girl..." He stopped speaking when she glanced over her shoulder at him. Her chestnut hair fell across one cheek and her eyes were sparkling in the sunlight.

It was no use. Nothing about this was going to get easy. If anything, looking into her eyes, he saw that not letting himself fall for Molly was going to be the hardest thing he'd ever done. Because he just realized that it was already too late.

When her lips curved into a tender smile and the edges of her eyes crinkled, he was done for. The surge of connection was so swift and strong it made the adrenaline rush he'd gotten as a bullfighter before meeting a two-thousand-pound angry bull feel like child's play.

"Is there something wrong?" she asked. He blinked at her in the morning sun.

Oh yeah, there was most definitely something wrong.

They were on Bob's back porch. She was collapsed in a lounge chair, filthy but content. John Boy was using her as a surfboard, tramping from her chest to her legs and back up again, tumbling on and off her as he went.

Bob was balanced on the porch railing, because though he'd made progress over the past few days, sinking down into a lounger was still an impossibility. He'd insisted on making sandwiches for them, saying that she'd gone beyond the call of duty by taking care of Baby One and Baby Two. She'd been too worn-out to argue and had listened to him maneuver slowly around in the kitchen. Sadly, she realized he didn't need her anymore. The man was very capable and resourceful.

Looking at him, she took a bite of her ham sandwich and thought about the "sadly" part. Sadly, he didn't need her. Sadly, she regretted that fact. Very much.

Baby One and Baby Two needed her though. Feeling conflicted and confused, she was inexplicably grateful for that. Of course, as soon as Baby One came around and started behaving, Bob would only need to hold the bottle through the fence and let them eat. Then she wouldn't be needed anymore by them either.

As a cloud of gray depression moved over her, she just did not understand what had happened to her. She had a plan. A plan she loved.

"Did anyone say last night if they'd figured out why Applegate and Stanley are mad at Sam?" she asked, more than ready to switch gears. She'd been wondering about the "feud" all week but had been too busy to look into it.

"I did hear someone say that Pete thought it had something to do with Adela."

That got Molly's investigative juices flowing. "What in the world could it be? I can't help it, I think at the shower today I'm going to ask some questions and see if I can come up with some answers. Last night when we sat at the table where they usually play checkers, it didn't feel right. You know, us being there and them not being around." Molly frowned. "And I can't help thinking part of the reason Sam's been so grumpy is because he misses his friends."

"You're the reporter," Bob said, setting his plate on the railing as he studied her for a minute. "Molly, for a while now I've been thinking about something you said that night at your apartment. When you cooked the lasagna, you said you hid in your closet. Why was that? Were you afraid? Or being punished?"

"No. Nothing like that," Molly said, startled by the question. She'd let that information slip out accidentally. She'd never discussed her past with anyone and had been relieved when he hadn't seemed to pick up on the reference that night. Obviously, he'd been listening. She took a deep breath. *Why not?* What was so traumatic about her past? Nothing that she couldn't talk about—at least with Bob.

She inhaled and met his questioning gaze. "You said

your father hadn't been there for you." Sitting up, she placed John Boy on the ground to explore and watched him for a second. "That he was always traveling. Well, my life was a little different, I lived with my parents in a middle-class neighborhood in Houston. To most people it looked like we had a perfect family. But my dad and mom had this love-hate thing going on and they argued constantly. As a child I couldn't understand it, and still don't really. I mean they loved each other, but they seemed to hate each other. When I was about four, I was playing with my dolls in my closet, pretending it was my dollhouse. That day when they started their usual round of fighting, for some reason I reached up and closed the door, muffling their angry words." Molly looked away from Bob, out to the clear summer day, with its soft breeze and uncomplicated open space. "It was unexplainable almost, sitting inside the darkness, trying to hide from their yelling…I don't remember being angry at them, I just remember disconnecting from their drama. I started daydreaming to block it all out. As a kid, it was my way of controlling my surroundings, I guess."

"How long did you do that? Hide in your closet like that."

She shrugged. "Years. At first I daydreamed because I found the dark soothing, like another buffer between the yelling. But as soon as I began to learn to write, I started turning on the light and journaling and it was like the light bulb came on inside of me. I became an observer during the day at school and a crazed diarist by night. Because there was always a fight between my parents, I got plenty of practice." She smiled at him, trying to reassure him that all was well—because it was, for her.

He didn't say anything for a moment. "I'm sorry."

"For what? You didn't do anything. And besides, I started early wanting to focus on stories about people and kids with real hardships. With real needs and hurts. I mean, after all, my home life might not have been perfect, but I had a roof over my head and food in my stomach."

"Then I guess on that matter, we're even," he said softly.

Molly nodded, feeling better somehow. "I guess so. You had a cross to bear that was different than mine, but linked. There are so many ways the world can break a person. I thank God that He entered my life when He did."

"Me, too. I was able to cope with the anger on my own, but it means the world to me to be free of it, although I find myself backtracking sometimes. When that happens God reminds me that He's freed me from it. My heart aches for those who haven't learned that God is the key to healing."

Molly thought about that, her mind churning. "I've toyed with writing a set of Bible studies on the subject of women transitioning from brokenness to healing. It was something I thought about right after I accepted the Lord, but I put it away. I mean, I'm not really qualified to produce something of that magnitude. You know I wouldn't want to lead anyone wrong. But, I could get qualified help, like Biblical advisors and a psychologist." She hadn't thought about it in a while. She'd written an article that skirted the issues, thinking it would appease the idea that had tugged at her heart right after she'd come to know the Lord. Nothing had been appeased, but the devotional was one of those things that had made her question the dream she was chasing. It was one of the things she'd become so adept at ignoring over time. She wasn't one of those people who could dream something all of her life and toss it away.

"What about your dream of travel? I wouldn't think there would be much travel involved in writing Biblical self-helps," Bob said.

"It was just a thought. You know how it is with me and ideas. I get them by the truckload..." She paused. Why did that suddenly sound so wrong?

Bob's lips flattened. "Yeah. I remember," he said, his eyes glinting in the sunlight. "Here, let me take your plate in. If you're going to make it to Dottie's wedding shower you need to head out."

Molly watched him go into the house. He'd moved so quickly that she almost forgot the cumbersome therapeutic boot on his left foot. Standing slowly, she followed him. Was it her imagination or was he irritated? "I'll come back out later to feed the babies. Can I bring you anything? Maybe some cake?"

"You're too sore to worry with those misfits today," he said gruffly. "I'll get one of the guys to come out and take care of it." He plunked the dishes into the sink. They clattered together, an unmistakable acknowledgment that all was not well.

"I can do it, Bob. I don't mind." What was wrong with him?

She stepped back when he swung around and glared at her. "Do what you want, Molly," he snapped. "I've got to do some paperwork I've been neglecting."

Molly watched him stalk down the hallway and into his office, closing the door behind him. She didn't have a clue about what had just transpired, but he'd gone from pleasant to angry in sixty seconds.

CHAPTER SIXTEEN

"Molly, dear, have you hurt yourself?"

Easing through the doorway of the convention center, Molly smiled at Adela, who was sitting beside the small table on which Dottie Hart's guestbook was displayed. Every muscle in Molly's body hurt. Including her heart. He'd shut her out. Or at least that's what it felt like. Funny thing was she'd never been *in*. Not really. All the time she'd been getting ready for the shower, her mind had been searching, wondering what had happened to upset Bob. She hadn't imagined it. He had been angry. Or upset.

They had been getting along so well. At one point during the afternoon she'd even thought...well, she thought he was going to kiss her. And she'd wanted him to. She'd wanted it so much it had startled her. But then in a flash everything had upended.

"I've been bottle-feeding two practically grown bulls."

Adela smiled, and her vivid blue eyes twinkled. "A delightful experience."

"You've done it?" She nodded and Molly could not picture Adela doing what she'd done today. There was not enough imagination in the world for her to picture Adela face-first in the dirt. "I bet you told them very sweetly to sit up and drink and they did exactly what you told them to do."

Adela smiled that serene smile of hers and patted the chair beside her. "After you've made the rounds, come and sit with me and I'll tell you all about it. I loved my babies."

"I would like that," Molly said.

The room was filled. Since Molly was running late, it seemed everyone had arrived ahead of her. She wasn't really a big conversationalist in crowds. She was a reporter. She observed. She set herself outside of herself and documented facts. She hugged Dottie, congratulated her on her upcoming marriage, then settled back with a cup of punch and took in her surroundings. To some it would look as if she was actually participating, but she wasn't.

She'd done it all her life. At home where it was better to be invisible. In high school, for a lonely girl without friends, reporting was a way of exploring other people's lives. Her writing was noticed by the teacher who oversaw the school paper. She'd been recruited and the little dream she'd first imagined while hiding in her closet as her parents fought started to take shape. For the first time, looking around the convention center, she didn't feel disconnected from everyone.

Lacy wouldn't let her, nor Sheri. It was like the first day she'd arrived in Mule Hollow. Those two had seen straight through her, as if recognizing that she was hiding inside the reporter shell. They didn't pressure her, but they loved to get her involved.

Molly knew that reaching out to people was Lacy's gift. Sheri credited Lacy with helping her overcome extreme shyness. And Lacy had done an outstanding job, because Sheri Marsh was now one of the most outspoken people Molly had ever met.

Molly scanned the room. Lilly Wells stood near the cake chatting with Norma Sue, who was holding Lilly's son, Joshua. That little baby was getting bigger every day. His cute little cherub cheeks were fat and rosy as he cackled at the face Norma Sue was making at him. Cassie was laughing with Esther Mae and Sheri.

Without even hearing any conversation, she knew it had to be an interesting one.

In the middle of the room stood Ashby Templeton and Rose Vinson. Tall and elegant, Ashby had moved to Mule Hollow at the same time as Molly to open her dress store. Rose was from the newly-established shelter No Place Like Home, and Molly had heard she'd just started working for Ashby.

Molly took a sip of her punch and met Adela's gaze as she scanned the room. She really wondered why Adela and Sam had never married. It was hard to think that the two long-time friends could just be shy. Or maybe they were scared.

Now wouldn't that be a quandary?

"Hey! You are in deep thought about something."

Molly almost dropped her punch, Lacy startled her so badly. "Didn't your mom ever teach you not to sneak up on a person?" She shot a fake glare at her friend.

"Believe me, my mama tried to teach me a lot of things that didn't stick. So tell me how it's going out there in Bob land."

Molly scowled for real at that. "That man is driving me crazy, Lacy."

Lacy beamed at her. "Really? Like *cra-a-zzy!*" she drew the word out and waggled her eyebrows at the same time. "Like Patsy Cline crazy?"

Molly glanced around to be sure no one else was within hearing distance. "Honestly, Lacy, yes." Now she'd admitted it to someone. And she knew she was not in her right mind, because she had admitted it.

Lacy rammed her orange fingernails into her windblown curls and Molly almost choked on the sip of punch she'd inhaled as Lacy barely contained the whoop of joy that came out as a very expressive whisper. Followed by a slap on the back! And sloshed punch. "Yep, yep, yep! I knew there was something between the two of you. I knew it. Of course I wasn't the only one—"

"Lacy," Molly hissed in a whisper. "Please get a hold of yourself. I said he was driving me crazy. There's an attraction. I didn't say I was giving in to it. Bob Jacobs is not looking for a woman like me. I don't meet any of the criteria that he's listed as his must-haves in a wife. Besides—"

"Christian," Lacy cut her off. "You meet the most important part. The two of you would be equally yoked. If you love the Lord and you love each other, what else is there? With those two points taken care of, anything else would be secondary."

"Not when two people are on separate continents." There—she'd got it out.

"Molly. You are not going to leave us. We need you. I know it. I know I do, Molly. I really do."

"Lacy. There are two problems with your theory.

One, who said Bob and I love each other? And two, I've been planning my entire life for a career as a journalist with some sort of connection to assignments overseas. I want to do work that has real potential to help change the world. And I'm hot right now. I know I have a real shot at three different openings and hope to hear something positive any day now."

"Look, Molly. I know you sent those résumés out and I know you're going to hear positive things back from them. Your work is wonderful and they'd be mad not to give you a job. But we need you here. Bob needs you. And others—have you not realized the people you influence with your column?"

They were starting to attract attention from others in the room and Molly didn't want to have everyone start in on her about staying in Mule Hollow. "Lacy. Shh. Everyone is looking and this is supposed to be about Dottie this afternoon."

Lacy plopped her hand to her jutting hip and cocked her head to the side, causing her hair to jiggle. "They all know, Molly. They've all watched you watching Bob sing in the choir on Sundays ever since you moved here. You are in love with the man."

"Lacy, that's ridiculous."

The entire room had slowly shifted closer to her. This wedding shower was supposed to be about Dottie, so why were they all watching her?

"Molly, you hang tough," Sheri called, raising her glass of sherbet punch and shaking her newly straightened brown hair. "Don't get married until you're ready. And if you want to travel and have a career then go for it. But run from this place. Run very, very fast."

"Sheri," Esther Mae gasped. "Don't tell her that. I know you think the fun ends at marriage, but you're wrong. Me and Hank always have fun."

Molly knew Esther Mae was talking to a wall when it came to Sheri getting married. She had no intentions of settling anytime in the near future. The girl loved dating and her freedom.

"Esther Mae, some of us just don't want to get tied down yet," Sheri said. "I never met a man I couldn't handle. I'm just trying to tell Molly that if she knows what she wants out of life, she should go for it. If I ever, in the really far-off future, find the man of my dreams, believe me, I will let nothing stand in my way to get him. But that is not happening anytime soon. I'm having a blast just as I am. But even so, I stopped drinking the water just in case." She jogged across the room and hugged Molly tight. It brought tears to Molly's eyes—because it hurt her sore muscles. "Remember, Molly, repeat after me, don't drink the water. There's something in it that makes you want to get married. And it's catching."

* * *

Bob limped into the dining room, carrying a metal garbage can firmly in his grasp. His world had been bonkers and it was time to set it right. Tossing the letters was the first thing. He wished the best for each and every woman who'd sent him a letter, but he had no desire to open them and he knew it wouldn't do him any good anyway. He wasn't interested.

Nope, for months now he'd pushed thoughts of Molly from his mind. He'd known early on that she wasn't the woman for him. There were too many things about her that just didn't fit…and yet he'd found himself right back to thinking about her when he let his guard down. He was on a collision course with heartbreak and he knew it.

It baffled him that she could write such admirable words about him and then not have any feelings for him.

But how could it get any plainer? The woman had gone so far as to start reading the letters. There were two neat stacks started. Two piles meant one thing. She was making him a yes and no pile.

Pathetic. Here he stood in a roomful of love letters

being screened by the woman who couldn't wait to marry him off to one of the authoresses, and what was he doing? Like a fool he was daydreaming about her! It was downright wrong.

Bending forward, ignoring the rupture of pain in his rib cage, he raked as much of the pile as would fit into the trash can. Then he headed outside.

It was time to put down his foot. Time to get his head on straight and put order back into his life.

"Bob!" Molly exclaimed, coming up behind him. He stood at the back past the barn, watching the fire in the burn-barrel. Before she asked, she knew what he was burning. Something in her head told her the moment she turned into his driveway and saw the smoke what was going on. He'd been angry before she left, but this? "Why?" she asked simply.

"Because I was tired of smelling them," he said, not bothering to turn around and look at her.

She was at a loss for words. After all, it was his business. She'd been out of line initiating the letters. But even with the nagging, sour feeling in her stomach, she'd had to acknowledge that there were some good ones mixed in there. Burning up with the rest of them.

A blast of anger swept through her and she started to open her mouth to tell him so, but clamped it shut instead. It wasn't for her to say what he did with the letters. It didn't matter that she wanted to say something so bad she could hardly stand it. She wasn't here to run his life. She was here to make up for a mistake, and the sooner she remembered that the better off she'd be. Anyway, it was obvious she was kidding herself.

Bob didn't need her anymore.

CHAPTER SEVENTEEN

Standing in the summer sun, feeling it warm her cold skin, Molly reminded herself she'd come here to make up for messing with Bob's life. It didn't matter that he'd told her he was glad it had given them time together. What did time together matter when in the end there was no place for it to go?

Spinning away while she had the fortitude, she walked back around the barn and down the length of fence until she came to the connecting pen where Baby One and Baby Two were corralled.

"How are my babies doing?" she said, not feeling the least bit enthused as she leaned over the fence and held out her hand. Baby Two was the first to come to her, and he nuzzled her open palm with his black nose. Despite her glumness, Molly laughed as a sudden feeling of contentment settled over her. It was the oddest thing. After a few seconds, Baby One must have felt left out, because he trotted over and bullied his way into the front. "Hey, play nice, little man." She rubbed the soft hair between his floppy ears and when Baby Two crowded up beside the fence, she reached out and scratched his forehead with her other hand. She was going to miss them. Bob's horse whinnied from his pen, wanting in on some of the action.

"Sorry, buddy, but I really don't know the first thing about what to do for you."

She said nothing when Bob walked up beside her. Molly refused to look at him, continuing instead to study Baby One and Two as she scratched their heads. She could see his profile from the corner of her eye and knew he was silently studying his horse. Tension hung around them. Obviously whatever had been wrong with him before she left for the shower hadn't righted itself. For Molly it was hard to stay mad at the man she wanted only the best for. The calves butted heads trying to be greedy with her touch so she pulled back and tucked her fingers in the pockets of her jeans. "Bob," she said, finally looking at him.

"Look, Molly, I..." He rammed his hands though his hair, and she was glad to see that he didn't flinch. "I didn't mean to make you mad. I know burning the letters probably hurt your feelings. I know you think my soul mate is in there, but she's not. And honestly, I don't want to think about that right now."

Molly closed her eyes. She didn't want to think about it, either. She was tired of thinking about it.

"You're not a horse person?"

His quiet question was a simple signal to let it go. Could she? She took a breath and met his gaze. She'd been so busy with the calves she hadn't given his big horse much thought. Clint or one of his hands had been taking care of his needs. "I've never been around them, being raised in the city like I was. And since I've been in Mule Hollow, I've not had an opportunity to be around them. You know, my writing keeps me busy." He nodded his head but didn't say anything. For a moment they both watched Clyde prance up and down the fence line trying to draw attention to himself.

"I think he misses you." Molly looked up at Bob again, her stomach tied in knots.

"Yeah, I know the feeling. Broken ribs or not, I'm going to have to take him for a ride soon. For my own enjoyment."

"But Clint can do that. You'll hurt yourself." No sooner were the words out than she wanted to kick herself. She was not his mother and he was obviously tired of everything, the matchmaking and being nursed. She closed her eyes and willed the protective nagging to go away. Her thoughts were so in need of a rest. "I'm sorry. I'm doing it again." She turned her back to him slightly and sighed. "You are a grown man and I cannot figure out why I keep interfering in your business. I've been thinking about it all day." It had become a constant in her life, this concern for him.

A gentle tug on a strand of hair had her looking over her shoulder. Bob had taken a step and was standing so close she could see the tiny flecks of baby-blue that fringed the midnight centers of his eyes. Her breath caught in her throat. Why did she care so much about Bob? She remembered the kiss, the gentle touch that she knew had no meaning to him. How could it when he hadn't even known he'd given it to her?

"Molly, your worrying doesn't bother me. It's nice. But…it's time for me to get back to work before I go any more stir-crazy. Tomorrow there's a private sale I've been planning to attend for weeks. I want to add to my stock, so I'm going."

Molly's instinct was to tell him he wasn't ready, but she bit her lip, instead. She'd known this was coming, that her time here was almost up. She just hadn't realized how much she wasn't ready to give it up. And now he was telling her he didn't need her anymore.

"Do you want to come?"

"What?" she gasped, completely shocked and

pleased by his question. It was a peace offering. Nothing more. But that didn't keep her heart from dancing. "Are you sure? I...I might try to baby you."

"No babyin' allowed," he said sternly, his eyes coming back to life as he grinned the trademark melt-your-heart smile of his.

"If you're sure. I could use the experience for an article."

"So is that a yes?"

She nodded. "Yes. I would love to go."

"Good." He studied her, more like the old Bob. "Come on." He took her hand, startling her with his touch.

He strode toward the barn and though he had the cumbersome orthopedic boot on his fractured leg, he hobbled along at a fast clip. And she was stumbling out of surprise.

"Where are we going?"

"I figure you might as well get all the firsthand experience you can while you're here."

"Okay, what does that mean?"

"You are going to ride my horse."

"What? I mean, I've never ridden a horse before."

"Then there's no time like the present to learn." Molly skidded on the cement, trying to get traction. "No. I can't."

He stopped in front of a saddle sitting on a rack and then walked over and opened the gate that Clyde had galloped up to as if he knew what was about to happen. The big brown horse let out a heavy breath and snapped his hooves to the ground in excitement. Molly stepped away. The horse was huge. Really big.

She was five-eight and yet she still had to raise her chin to look into his eyes. And he was staring at her.

"I, uh, no."

Bob laughed at her inability to verbalize her objection.

"For a reporter you do have a way with words."

"Not fair. I can't—"

"'Can't' never could do anything. Don't you know that?"

Molly watched as he pulled a thick multicolored horse blanket off the wooden fence and laid it over Clyde's back. The big horse didn't move a muscle, just kept right on staring into Molly's eyes. "They can sense fear, can't they?" she asked, knowing that if it was true, this horse had her number.

"You'll do fine, Molly. I'm going to be right beside you."

She noticed that he didn't answer her question. But she knew the horse knew she was scared. Clyde blinked his long lashes and leaned his head to the side, watching her. He did have the most beautiful chocolate-colored eyes. And those lashes were to die for. Maybe he wouldn't be so bad.

Bob lifted the saddle and she heard his sharp intake of breath. "See, you're hurting yourself. You should not be doing this." She moved to take part of the weight of the saddle and ended up helping him place it on Clyde's back.

"Thank you."

She was dismayed that he was hurting himself and that she'd actually helped in her own demise. She gaped at him as he grunted when he reached for the girder or the girdle—she didn't know what the thing was called, but she knew it was the important part, because it held the saddle on the horse's back. Wringing her hands together as one, she pointed. "Do it tight," she instructed. That got her an insolent look.

"Relax, Molly. Do you trust me?" Molly hesitated.

"Ha!" he laughed. "You wrote all those nice things about me and told almost the entire world what a wonderful catch I was and you don't trust me! I'm devastated." He laid his right hand over his heart and batted his beautiful navy eyes.

Smiling, she poked his arm. "Yes, I trust you. You jumped to conclusions."

"You hesitated."

They were standing close staring at each other. Molly could see the edges of his lips quiver and felt the response of her own. They burst into laughter simultaneously. Of course she could tell Bob immediately regretted it when his expression crashed from grinning to a grimace of pain instantly.

Molly covered her cheeks with her palms, then clamped her lips together to try and get control of herself. Watching him in pain was not the time to dissolve into giggles.

"What are we going to do now? You refused the last batch of letters forwarded from the newspaper and now you've burned up all the perfectly good wedding proposals. Your mailbox has been stolen and there is no more cake in your kitchen. What am I going to do with you?"

Bob reached for the halter and trailed a hand down Clyde's neck. "I don't know what you're going to do about me, but I'm going to give you your very first horseback lesson. And forget about all that other. Remember."

Molly realized that she was looking forward to riding lessons from Bob.

Watching his gentleness with Clyde and the way the big horse trusted him, Molly knew she had nothing to fear as long as Bob was beside her. She did trust him. It was something she'd known even before he'd rescued her from Sylvester.

She'd known from the first day she'd met him.

CHAPTER EIGHTEEN

"So how's the weather up there?" Bob said, as he halted Clyde with the simple touch of his hand to the big horse's forehead. Molly had done very well. She had a natural seat in the saddle, which made learning to ride that much easier.

But she was already beat-up enough from the calves. He didn't want her not to be able to walk tomorrow because her first lesson had gone on too long.

Still, he was reluctant to end the lesson. They'd relaxed and things were flowing easily between them again. For the moment. He wasn't certain why he'd even offered the lesson. Who was he kidding—he hadn't offered it—he'd talked her into taking the lessons. But while he'd been burning those letters, all he could think about was how much she would enjoy learning more about his way of life.

"I love it! I really do think I could grow to love this."

Leading Clyde to the stall, Bob moved to help her dismount. "Like I told you—"

"I know, I know," Molly cut in, grinning. "This cowboy life can be addictive."

"Out of the mouth of babes comes the truth."

She made a face at him but made no move to dismount. "Bob, could I write about learning to ride and also about the wild experience of feeding Baby One and Baby Two? I wouldn't have to mention your name if you don't want me to. I can just mention a really wonderful cowboy who helped me."

Looking up at her, he figured in that moment, with the happiness written all over her face, he'd have said yes to anything. "Actually, I look forward to reading what you have to say on both subjects." Truth of the matter was her articles had actually done something nice for him. He'd meant it when he'd told her that he was glad he'd had the chance to enjoy her company.

"Awesome. Thank you. I really think my readers will get a kick out of it. Just like I have."

He watched as she swung her leg over Clyde's back and stepped down, holding on to the saddle horn for stability. "It shows. Look at how well you did that. I thought you hadn't ridden before."

She bit her lip and looked disarmingly sheepish. "I

watch television and they always do it that way."

"Oh yeah. The good ol' TV. What would we do without it?"

"I think we would probably do very well."

"I agree," he said. "Just think what kids are missing."

"You want lots of children, don't you?" She reached to help him lift the saddle from Clyde.

He picked up a grooming brush. "I do. I can't help myself. I want kids. I want little girls and I want little boys. Just thinking about them makes good things happen in my heart." He paused, brushing Clyde's coat down, and looked at Molly. She was watching him with an expression he couldn't read. "I believe God equips us for the task that He puts before us. I think being a lonely kid basically without parents has equipped me to be a great parent and husband. Because I want it so much, family is something I'll never take for granted." He let the brush run down Clyde's flank, thinking hard about all that had transpired during the course of the day.

"You'll be a great father."

Molly's quiet assurance meant a lot to him. He met her gaze.

"You would be a great mother." It was sad that she didn't want kids. Sad in more ways than one, sad that they had such different outlooks on life. He wished... Molly shook her head. "I don't think I have it in me."

"Sure you do."

"No."

Her reaction surprised him. He'd thought she didn't want children because of her career choice. Could it be she really believed she wouldn't be a good mother? "Molly, you were ferociously determined to take care of Baby One and Two. I mean, sweetheart, you did not take failure as an option. And then you bonded with them. Now I know they aren't children, but they do show how strong the mothering instinct is inside of you. And now you want to brag to the world about what fun you had doing it. I think that's wonderful."

His smile was meant to encourage her. She looked away from him, but not before he saw what looked suspiciously like longing.

"It's strange," she said hesitantly, lifting her hand to rub Clyde's neck. "In many ways our childhoods were similar. I mean, you were raised in a boarding school without your parents and I was raised at home with both my parents there, yet I was just as alone as you. Do you see that?"

He nodded. From what she'd told him she'd lived a very isolated life. She still lived an isolated life. He wondered if she realized the kind of lifestyle she was aiming for. Always the observer, rarely the participant. It wasn't good for her. He'd enjoyed pulling her away from that solitude. It would be his pleasure to continue to draw her out. But if she truly had wanderlust in her blood, as his father'd had, nothing would hold her back. He had been struggling to understand God's reasoning for what had been happening in his life over the past week. He'd run the gamut of emotional feelings. He was at a point of no return, something he wasn't ready to look straight in the eye. But he was praying that the Lord would lead. For both of them.

Molly let her hand drop from Clyde's neck and walked away.

"Good boy," he whispered to Clyde. He patted his horse on the rump, watched him trot out into the round pen, and only then did he dare trust himself to follow Molly.

She was standing at the entrance of the barn staring out toward his house. Framed in the double door opening of the barn, she looked small and starkly alone. His chest ached for her, and it had nothing to do with his broken ribs. He limped to stand behind her, fighting off the urge to reach out to her, something he'd wanted to do all afternoon. But he kept his hands away, tucking them into his pockets instead.

"Molly, what are you afraid of?"

"Making the wrong choice." She reached to twine her fingers in the chain around her neck, a movement as natural to her as sticking the pencil behind her ear each morning, but instead she let her hand fall back to her side.

Her revelation stunned him. "I thought you knew exactly what you wanted out of life," he blurted out, stepping closer to her.

She shook her head. "Not anymore. Honestly, I'm so confused, I…"

Bob's heart kicked up, and before he could stop himself he took her arm gently and tugged her around to look at him. The emotion in her eyes spoke to a hope inside him.

"Molly," he started, not certain what words were forming in his mind, which was still reeling from the sudden impact of her admission.

"Don't." She lifted her hand to his lips, shook her head then hurried away.

He let her go. His heart was pounding the chant that he should stop her. Yet his mind was listing alphabetically the reasons why the hope in his heart wouldn't work.

Fear. That's what she felt. Sheer, get-me-out-of-this-tight-space kind of fear. Her heart was pounding as if she'd just dropped fifty stories in an elevator without cables. When Bob had talked about kids, something inside of her had charged to life. She'd never let herself think about kids. Her life as a child hadn't given her any maternal instincts. Nothing had. She admitted that honestly. Lilly and Cort's baby, Joshua, was the cutest little boy she'd ever laid eyes on—and she even enjoyed holding him for about two whole minutes—but to actually be a parent hadn't crossed her mind. Mostly because, one, she figured she'd be lousy at it and, two, she was scared of it. What if she didn't have the instinct? Her parents hadn't had the natural instinct. Either that, or they just didn't care about it. Things were genetic. What if she was like them?

And what about travel? She would never do to her child what Bob's dad had done to him. Poor Bob. To have lost his mother at a young age, through death, and then to lose his dad to a career choice. It was horrible, but it happened every day.

Molly chose not to have children if she couldn't commit to them. What was she saying—she'd chosen not to have a husband, either.

Her hands were shaking when she started her car and drove away from Bob. She could see him in her rearview watching her until she drove over the hill that protected his house and barn from view of the road. She'd run away. Like a child!

She crossed the cattle guard, and turned toward Mule Hollow and sanity. Maybe. In her mind she backtracked, trying to come to some kind of determination of what was happening to her.

She had only begun to feel the love of a father after coming to know the Lord as her personal Savior. Things had been changing since that day in Lacy's salon where she gave her life to Christ. Feelings that had been locked inside her heart were coming out, and sometimes she didn't handle them well. Sometimes she didn't know what to do with them. Like reservations about her dreams. Dreams she'd had since childhood. Dreams that had sustained her through disappointments and sorrows. Doubts that she'd continually denied, pushed back into the shadows.

She'd spent her entire life meeting one goal after the other, which would eventually lead her to the faraway places she'd dreamed of. The streets of Brazil. The jungles of Africa. Dreams that would take her to the stories she wanted to tell.

Or were they dreams that would simply help her escape?

She needed to seek the Lord in prayer. Needed His holy guidance. There was a tug-of-war going on in her heart and she knew only God could lead her to still waters. She just had to trust Him. And hear His words when He spoke.

It was nine o'clock when she walked into her apartment and dropped her backpack on the couch. Her head was still spinning as she walked through the small, dark living room and into the kitchen. Turning on the light above the stove, she filled a small pan with water, then went to her room and made quick work of showering off the smell of horse, cows and dirt. Not very glamorous, but so completely satisfying.

The water was boiling in the pan when she made it back to the kitchen. She sighed, pouring it over the bag of green tea she'd placed in the bottom of her cup. The room was quiet as she methodically took the string and let the tea bag swim in the cup. The clock seemed to pound out the passing seconds as Molly glanced around the tiny apartment softly lit by the glow of the single bulb above the stove. She was struck emphatically by the aloneness and isolation that surrounded her. She'd been isolated all her life. Was this really the life she wanted?

Right now the only thing she was certain of was that she wanted to go to the auction with Bob tomorrow. And it had nothing at all to do with writing research.

She was taking a sip of tea when she noticed the

blinking light on her answering machine.

Bob pretty much held his breath waiting to see if Molly was going to show up to go to the auction. When her yellow car topped the hill, he breathed a sigh of relief.

He'd wanted her to come. It was good for her to be getting out and experiencing new things. Any other reasons he had for being glad to see her he pushed away as secondary and not up for debate. Today was about getting Molly involved in something other than what she could create with her fingers and a computer. No analyzing, no thinking about why and why not. He simply wanted to spend the day with Molly. He *needed* to spend the day with Molly.

She pulled to a halt beside the truck and smiled when he opened the door for her.

"I'm glad you came," he said, happy when she took the hand he offered her. Her eyes met his and she hesitated, then gave him a wavering smile. She had on jeans and a soft green shirt that set off her eyes. As usual her beauty tugged at him, especially since he'd come to know the person behind the beauty was so undeniably wonderful.

"I couldn't pass up a chance like this," she said. "But

what about Baby One and Two? Do I need to feed them before we go?"

And she thought she wouldn't make a great mother. "I rigged them a stationary feeder, so you don't have to get dirty before we go."

"Oh."

He was surprised by her reply. "But you can feed them this evening." That got him a smile. He wondered if something more was bothering her. She seemed unsettled.

"I'd like that," she half laughed. "I've grown attached to the little monsters."

"I do believe, Miss Popp, that we can make a cowgirl out of you yet." He opened the door of the truck for her then closed it behind her. By the time he made it around and had climbed into the driver's seat, the truck interior already smelled of the soft scent of flowers that he'd come to associate with Molly.

"You don't even act like your leg hurts. That amazes me."

Maybe he'd just imagined that something was bothering her, he thought as he checked his mirrors then pulled out of the yard. "Believe me, compared to the way my ribs felt in the beginning, the leg doesn't hurt at all. The boot is pretty cool, it takes all the weight. Problem is, I haven't figured out how to get a spur on it."

Molly laughed and Bob had never felt more right. He knew if he could spend the rest of his life making Molly laugh, his life would be perfect.

Today was going to be all about showing Molly his world. Of course it had been nagging at him ever since he'd asked her to come what he thought he was going to accomplish by this. She would be leaving and he would be heading down a road to heartbreak.

The jolt of the cattle guard made his ribs feel as if they were grinding together, but one look at Molly and he didn't feel a thing. He would take what he could get. As they sped down the road toward Ranger, Molly seemed distracted. He chalked it up to her writing and the way her mind worked. He told himself she was thinking about a story. After all, he'd witnessed her nearly bump into walls during all the months he'd watched her scribbling in that pad she kept in her back pocket. Her ever-present stories… He was jealous. He admitted it.

He wanted a wife who was into him and the children they would have. So what was all this about? Was it so wrong that he'd wanted the day to be about Molly and getting her involved in something other than writing? Not that she hadn't been completely up front about why she'd come.

She'd said she could use the experience for her writing. So why had he foolishly thought it would be any other way?

Pushing aside his disappointment, he focused on her. Despite everything, he was going to enjoy the day. If it killed him.

He prayed for God to show him the way. He prayed for some answers.

Though she didn't seem fully engaged in her surroundings, Molly started asking questions about cattle and auctions specifically. Conversation helped ease the tension between them. The way she was drilling him with questions, he figured she'd be a seasoned pro when they finally arrived.

While he, on the other hand, was reminded that she loved what she did.

It was a part of her that would always be there. Listening to her ask questions, he thought about all the times since he'd known her, how he'd been drawn to her. And suddenly, like a bucket of ice water in the face, he saw that the part of her he'd thought he couldn't live with was, in fact, one of the things about her that intrigued him and drew him to her.

Her commitment, her excitement about her writing, her determination—they were all attributes he admired. They were all qualities that made Molly who she was. And despite everything he'd gone through with his dad's rejection, he couldn't help loving her.

Molly knew she'd talked nonstop all the way to the cattle auction, but she hadn't been able to stop herself. Her nerves were shot, had been ever since she'd pushed the button on her answering machine and heard the words she'd waited all her life to hear.

At first she replayed the message four times, standing beside the machine with one hand over her mouth. *World View* magazine wanted to interview her at their office in New York. They were considering one other candidate, but the personal quality that Molly brought to her work had them looking at her in a highly positive light. Plus, the overseas travel was extensive, making the job well suited to a person with no qualms about being on the move. According to her résumé, she met all qualifications perfectly and should expect things to go well for her in the final interview phase.

By the fourth time she played the recording, she knew something was wrong. After years of dreaming about a job like this, she'd expected, even anticipated, her reaction would be one of overwhelming excitement and joy. She'd initially felt it during the first listen through. But then reality had set in, and everything that would occur if she took the job came crashing in around her.

She would have to leave Mule Hollow, which she'd known all along. She'd been prepared to leave it behind from the very beginning. Why then was this sense of mourning suddenly giving her second thoughts? Molly started pacing the living room.

She'd worked so hard for this. She wanted it with all of her heart. Sought it. And she would have it.

By the time she'd crawled into bed and turned off her lights, she'd thanked God for leading her and giving her the opportunity of a lifetime. All that was left before she flew out on Sunday was to tell Bob.

Why was it so hard? Just tell him!

She kept telling herself that as they wandered from pen to pen and he explained his reasons behind his bid on each bull, steer or heifer he chose from the masses. It was a lovely day and the auction wasn't exactly what she'd expected. It was very impressive, extravagant actually, and she realized early on that Bob wasn't just buying any cattle. He was purchasing top-quality stock to build a life on.

A life for the family he wanted.

By the time they were heading home, Molly didn't care to talk anymore. Bob on the other hand took up the slack and was exposing more of his plans for his ranch. He seemed totally and completely unaware that she'd shut down. Molly realized it was because he was looking toward his future, his dream. The dream that was so far removed from hers, she was out of her element even thinking about it.

All was quiet when they pulled into the yard and Bob backed the trailer up to the pen where the new purchases would spend their first night on his property. While he went to let them out of the trailer, Molly hurried to her car. Her heart was heavy, aching as it had been all day. With every mile they'd come closer to home, she had fought back tears. And all she wanted now was to get away.

"Molly," Bob said, startling her as he tapped her on the shoulder. "Where are you going?"

She turned toward him. They were standing in the square of light cutting a path across the yard from the open double doors of the barn.

"I'm going home, Bob. I had a very nice day…"
Coward!

"Molly, what's wrong? You've been quiet all the way here. Talk to me."

"No." She swung away from him, unable to look in his eyes. But she owed it to him to be up front. Slowly she turned around and met his solid gaze. "What am I doing here, Bob? What are we doing here?"

He took a step toward her, cupping his palm around the back of her neck and gently tugging her toward him. "I stopped asking that question halfway home, Molly. All I know is that we're here. For reasons I can't fully comprehend, we are here."

He searched her eyes. Molly's heart was beating uncontrollably and her throat felt as if it would explode with the effort of holding back the tears welling within it.

Bob wrapped her in his embrace and slowly lowered his lips to hers. His eyes met hers just before their lips touched and Molly thought her legs would buckle from the emotion warring in his beautiful eyes. In his powerful arms, his heart racing against hers, Molly thought she could stay in the moment for the rest of her life. And for an instant the world disappeared as he pulled her closer and deepened the kiss. His hand came up to cup her jaw as if she were a delicate flower and she sighed against his lips. It was such a gentle and sweet gesture and the kiss was so full of promise that it broke Molly. Suddenly she realized that this was the Miss Right kiss—the one she'd wanted but dared not hope for. With that thought a tear slipped down her cheek before she could stop it.

It was a heartfelt wish come true, but she knew now, nothing could ever really be between them. She could never be the woman of his dreams.

She could never be the traditional housewife and mother that he so fervently wanted. There were so many things against it. It would never work and she knew it.

Her heart was pounding and every fiber in her body was fighting her as she gently pushed against his shoulder breaking the kiss. "I have something to tell you. I'm leaving for New York the day after tomorrow. I—" She forced lightness into her heart that she didn't feel. After all she was going after her dream, this was the best for both of them. "I have an interview with *World View*. It's everything I've worked for. Everything I've dreamed of."

Bob blinked. His nostrils flared as he sucked in a deep breath. "I see," he said, looking at his boots. "It's a done deal?" His gaze met hers.

Molly shifted from one foot to the other. "Pretty much. One other candidate, but they said the odds were in my favor."

He gave a curt nod, sucking in a deep breath. "It was inevitable, your dreams coming true. You deserve it." Molly smiled but didn't feel it. He wasn't even trying to hold her back. What had she expected? They had become close over the past few days…maybe not as close as she'd thought. If he was feeling the strain she was feeling, wouldn't he at least try to hold her back? Or maybe he just understood better than she did that no matter how many kisses they shared, they were still worlds apart when it came to anything lasting that could connect them.

Why did that make her want to cry? "Well, I need to go," she managed. "You'll be okay?"

He nodded, blinking. "Yeah. Like I told you. It's time for me to get back to my life."

She took a step, toward her car. "Yes. You do need to do that." She stopped backing up. "I had fun. This week."

He nodded. "Me, too."

She spun away and hurried inside her car. "Molly."

"Yes." She looked back, a thrill of expectation slicing through the darkness in her heart.

"Good luck."

"Oh." What had she been expecting? "Yes, th-thank you."

CHAPTER NINETEEN

Adela patted the chair beside her. "Come. Sit with me before you go."

Molly set her suitcase down on and eased into a wicker chair beside the matching one that Adela was sitting in on her front porch. Molly had been so overwhelmed at the shower that they hadn't had a chance to talk.

"What scares you, Molly?"

Molly didn't want to hear that question anymore—she didn't really know the answer.

Adela laid a delicate hand on her arm. "I've been watching you and reading your articles since you moved here. You write about how wonderful Mule Hollow is and you write about all the successful weddings we've had, yet I sense there is a part of you that doesn't believe."

"Believe?"

Adela leaned her head slightly and her smile saddened. "You don't believe...in..."

She studied Molly for the longest moment, and Molly felt as if the deepest secrets of her heart were being exposed. Her heart began pounding, and she felt her palms begin to sweat.

"...you don't believe in happily ever after."

Molly looked down at her hands, unable to see the truth reflected in Adela's eyes. Unable to sit, she stood and started pacing. Storming to the end of the porch, she stared down Main Street, then she whirled around and stalked back to where Adela sat patiently, her hands folded in her lap. Her expression was one of patience. Molly ran a hand through her hair then grabbed the chain at her neck. "I see the hope of happily ever after." She let her hand drop and slap herself on the thigh. "But then I look around and I don't know, Adela. Is it just something that really only a few lucky people actually achieve? I mean here in Mule Hollow there is a sense that love can survive. It's one of the things that drew me here. But out there—" she let her hand fly out in an arch "—I don't know. It's like everything has to be perfect in order for love to make it through all the garbage that the world throws at two people. I can't even begin to figure out my folks' problems. They just didn't work. Whatever the great common denominator to a happy marriage was, they didn't get it. It's so easy for some people." She was rambling, she knew it, but there was a lot to get out. It was as if now that she'd started talking about it, she couldn't stop the flow. Everything wanted out.

"Molly, there is a common denominator. The Lord."

"True. That's the way it's supposed to be, but I see Christian marriages fall apart every day, too. It's not as easy for most people as it was for you. Or for Norma Sue or Esther Mae."

"So you think my marriage was easy? Molly, most marriages take a lot of hard work and focus. I think that one of the reasons so many fall apart is that it *is* hard work. Even for people who love the Lord."

Molly sank into the chair again, remembering all the harsh words she'd heard her parents yelling over the years.

"Molly."

"Yes, ma'am." She looked up from her hands to see Adela smiling.

"I can't tell you why every marriage doesn't work. There are too many variables, but if a couple puts God at the head of their household, and if a man and a woman love each other unselfishly, seeking God's will first, then they can have a beautiful life together. And so much fun and joy. Believe me, there is enduring love out there. Life is much more when you can walk hand in hand with the one you love."

Molly sighed. "Oh Adela, I'm so confused. After all these years I have the opportunity for the career that I've always wanted, or thought I wanted until I fell in love with Bob." She loved Bob Jacobs.

The realization stunned her. It wasn't as if it had blindsided her. It was more that it always had been there. Like the way Bob had shown her to ease into the saddle on her first horse ride, she'd eased into understanding that what she felt for Bob was love. "But there are so many things that make it impossible." She spoke the words to Adela, but also to herself. Just because she acknowledged that she loved him didn't suddenly make everything in her world right.

"Nonsense. Nothing is impossible. Two people just have to seek God and then work together to make it happen."

Molly wasn't so sure of that. "Can I ask you a personal question?"

Adela nodded, her blue eyes full of encouragement. "What about you and Sam? I mean, I've been watching you and I know you love each other."

Adela's smile faltered and she looked down the road toward Sam's Diner. "I've loved Sam always as my friend. He's more dear to me than anyone on earth and he's loved me always." She paused, thinking. "Molly, I'll share this with you because maybe it will help you. Maybe that's why God set this meeting up. Sam is a stubborn man. Full of pride and fear. I would marry him in a minute because I truly believe that God has blessed me with loving not once, but twice in my lifetime. But my Sam." Her smile broadened. "My Sam, I think, fears that I could never love him like I loved Theo. Deep in his heart, he's jealous of the love we shared. I think he's afraid to have faith that our love can be as special."

Molly couldn't miss the sadness in Adela's voice as her smile faded. Forgetting her own worries, she scooted to the edge of the chair and reached for Adela's hand. Such a wise and loving woman.

"Have you spoken to him about this?"

The older woman squeezed her hand tightly. "No dear. I can't fight Sam's fight for him. He must work through his own faith and come to realize that God blessed us with each other. I pray that one day he will wake up and trust my love enough to ask me to marry him. But even if he never does, it doesn't change my love. It is here for him. Patiently waiting." She patted Molly's hand. "Now, you should go. You don't want to miss that plane."

HOLD ME, COWBOY

Glancing at her watch, Molly was surprised at how time had flown. It was true, if she was going to catch her flight she needed to get on the road now. Reaching out, she hugged Adela. "Thank you. I'll see you when I get back."

Picking up her suitcase, she placed it in the back seat, her heart feeling heavier than the case. Her dreams were on the verge of coming true and all she could think about was Bob.

"Adela," she said, before closing her door. Adela smiled. She was standing on the steps, her hands folded together, watching Molly. "Pray for me."

She nodded. "I am."

CHAPTER TWENTY

Bob pulled his truck to a stop in front of Sam's. It was nine o'clock in the morning and he'd decided he couldn't take the solitude of his ranch any longer. Molly had only been gone for three days and it seemed like a lifetime. Now, sitting in front of the diner, he wasn't sure why he'd come. It wasn't just anyone's company he sought. It was Molly's and she wasn't here.

And you might as well get used to it.

He yanked on the handle and shoved the door open, not feeling the pain in his ribs because it was overshadowed by the pain in his heart.

Walking through the heavy door and into the ancient diner, his mind in turmoil, he didn't even realize he'd walked into the middle of a private moment until it was too late to disappear. Applegate was standing by the counter with his checkerboard tucked under his arm, while Stanley stood beside him holding their five-pound bag of sunflower seeds locked in the crook of his arm. Sam stood behind the counter with a scowl on his weathered face as he listened to what Applegate was saying. Bob hadn't been thinking about fireworks when he made the stop, but he couldn't very well back out the door now that he was there.

"Just because I called you on the fact that you're being ignorant is no call for you to run us outta here," Applegate said, his frown drooping like a hound dog's. "That's right. We were just doin' what friends do,"

Stanley agreed. "We watch *Dr. Phil,* you know."

"And *Oprah,*" snapped Applegate.

"Friends are supposed to tell the truth," Stanley continued.

Sam didn't look too convinced. Bob wanted to go, but his interest got the better of him and he took a step away from the door. After all, he'd do anything to not think about Molly.

"Bob," Sam grumbled. "Come on in here. Applegate and Stanley were just about to leave and quit disruptin' my business."

He looked pointedly at them.

"We weren't goin' anywhere," Applegate said, and to prove it, he walked over to his table and slapped his checkerboard down, then whirled around and went back to the counter. "This here's an inter-ven-chin."

"That's exactly what it is," Stanley said. Following Applegate's lead he walked over and plopped the sunflowers down beside the checkerboard, sending a couple of dozen shooting out of the top and skidding across the floor.

"An *inter-what?*" Sam snapped, snatching up the coffeepot and making Applegate take a step back. Bob thought that was a smart idea seeing how Sam looked like he might toss it on him.

"An intervention," Applegate said, thrusting his bony chest out. "You know the thang friends do when their friend ain't usin' the brain God gave 'im and needs his friends to think for him."

Sam growled. "If the two of you think I'll ever need yer kind to do any thinkin' fer me then you're both crazier than Art Holboney was the day he tried to get Norma Sue to marry him so's she could fix his tractors!"

"Hey, no need to get mean," Stanley yapped. "Art Holboney was dumber than dirt."

"Exactly," Sam snapped back, never losing a beat. Bob stepped close, his orthopedic boot and his cowboy boot beating an uneven rhythm on the wood floor as he crossed the room in the sudden silence. "Look, fellas, I don't know what's going on between the three of you, but this is no way to handle it." Why had he come to town? Why hadn't he stayed on his ranch? Town was getting wackier by the day. "Would anyone like to let me in on what's come between all of you?" He looked from one to the other, but they'd clammed up. "You want some coffee?" Sam asked, lifting a cup from its rack and pouring before Bob said yes.

"It's not ours to tell," Applegate said. With the wind now out of his sails, he sounded deflated. "We're just going to sit over here and play our checker game and show our support."

Sam glared at Applegate, who lifted his hands in a no-contest palms-out gesture. "That comes straight out of the Good Book, so don't you be giving me that look no more."

"We'll be right over here if you need to talk," Stanley said, and followed Applegate to the table by the window.

"By the way," Applegate said, turning back. "This matchmaking thang has been hard on me and Stanley. And other than showing support fer Sam, we figure we're gonna let the womenfolk take care of things like this from here on out. So, Bob, we'll be bringing back yer mailbox this afternoon. We figured to try and get you and Molly some alone time...you know the TV shows talk about the need fer quality time, so's we figure the best way of givin' you and Molly that time—you know, so you both could come to yer senses—was to make sure them other women couldn't find ya. Seein' how some folks was giving out yer address and all. But we're done. If'n you and Sam are gonna both play dumb, then Stanley and me figure we can't do you no good." That said, he heaved a sigh and sat down at the table, effectively shutting everything out but his game.

Bob was stunned. App and Stan stealing his mailbox? *Matchmaking?* This town was getting weirder by the minute.

"They've lost what few marbles God gave 'em in the first place," Sam grunted.

Bob put what they'd said to him out of his mind and turned back to Sam. He wasn't clear on what had happened between the three older men, but he had to agree with Sam on that assumption. Sliding onto a stool, he took a sip of his coffee, hoping it would clear his mind. "Well, son." Sam cleared his throat and studied the floor before looking at him. "You're the last person I expected to see here."

"Why's that? I needed a cup of coffee." He didn't know how he was supposed to handle all of this. Was Sam going to act as if nothing had happened just now?

And was Bob supposed to go along with it? Taking another drink of his coffee, he asked the Lord to do the intervention, because he didn't know what was wrong with Sam. He did know that Applegate and Stanley were right. If Sam needed them, then his friends needed to step up to the plate and help him. Was he sick? He didn't look sick. He looked sad. They'd said matchmaking. Were they trying to help Sam out with Adela?

Agitated, Sam snatched up a dishrag and started wiping down the spotless countertop, glancing toward the window where his buddies were happily jumping checkers. If anybody else had walked through that door, they'd never believe what Bob had just witnessed. Everything looked normal.

Like he'd run out of steam, in slow motion Sam stopped wiping the counter, slapped the rag across his shoulder and met Bob's gaze. "I figured ya fer a smart one. I figured you'd be on a plane to New York." He rubbed his chin.

"What?" Bob took a sip of coffee to hide his surprise as his stomach knotted.

"You heard me. You got yer whole life ahead of ya and an open opportunity, and you're gonna let Molly get away. I don't get it. It's you that needs the intervenin'. Not from them two crazy coots over thar though." His eyes narrowed. "Look, son, I've lived my life behind this counter and I'm tellin ya, looking back, I agree with App and Stanley. I'm a fool, a coward."

It was Bob's turn to narrow his eyes. "What in the world are you talking about, Sam? You're neither of those things. And if they're your friends, they'd never have said such a thing." He glared toward the window. Either App's and Stanley's hearing aids were down too low for them to hear or they were pretending not to hear, as they were known to do.

"Look, alls I'm sayin' is life ain't that long. And if you've got the chance of having a little bit of God's grace while you're livin' here, then go get it. Don't let that girl get away 'cause of yer pride."

Bob hung his head. "Sam, it doesn't have anything to do with my pride. Even if I thought Molly loved me, which I don't, going after her isn't the answer. If I thought loving me would be enough then it might be the answer. But this is about Molly. Right now she has a chance at achieving her dream…and it's because I love her that I can't try to stand in the way of that. At the same time, I can't wish that her dreams fall through—that wouldn't be any kind of love. So basically I'm in a hole without a shovel."

Sam looked thoughtful. "Sadly, I can understand that correlation." He looked toward the window once more and shook his head, blowing out a huff of pent-up air. "My Adela, she loved Theo Ledbetter more'n anything. Forty years ago, even if I'd had the courage to ask her to marry me before he popped the question, it wouldn't have done me a spec of good. She only had eyes for Theo and everybody knew it. Marrying someone by default ain't exactly the happily ever after a person dreams about."

Bob had to agree with Sam. He'd never liked being second choice in anything.

The elevator doors slid open with a soft whoosh barely audible over the excited chatter of the three children standing with their parents at the front of the crowded lift. Molly stood at the back of the elevator and waited for everyone else to exit. Why had she come? She was not the best at heights and her one true love was not waiting out there on the landing for her. So what in the world had possessed her to stand in line for thirty minutes to make the stomach-tingling ride to the top of the Empire State Building?

She didn't have a clue.

"Ma'am, are you going or staying?"

She smiled at the dignified older man holding the door for her. "I'm staying. Thank you."

She stepped out onto the tile then moved to the double doors leading onto the deck of the historical building.

The magnificent lighted view took her breath away, but since she really wasn't that fond of heights, she stayed close to the walls and didn't venture over to the fenced outer edge. All around her families were exchanging excited conversations about the view. A mother was holding her little girl's hand, pointing at various illuminated landmarks. A father stood at the corner of the building and took his son into his arms so that he could see through the viewfinder. Their heads were bent close, their dark curls mingling as they took in the sight together.

Molly swallowed a lump in her throat. She was standing at the top of the world and she had never felt so alone in all of her life.

Why had she come?

A woman passed by. She was alone, self-assured and, unlike the picture Molly was certain she was portraying, the woman looked happy and content. She was snapping pictures with her palm-size digital camera, totally engrossed in what she was doing. Alone but connected to what was going on around her.

Molly was an observer. That was what she did. She disconnected and then created her own illusion of the truth of the story she was writing.

So why had she left the interview, climbed into a taxi and come to the Empire State Building? Nostalgia?

Because in your heart of hearts you wish Bob had been here waiting.

Molly walked to the stone wall and wrapped her fingers around the chain-link fencing that rose from the top of it. The cold steel fencing was a safety precaution. It kept people from harming themselves. It let people observe the incredible view without worry. Kind of the way Molly had viewed life through the viewfinder of her writing. Always the observer, seldom the participant.

* * *

Bob was standing in front of Sam's Diner when he saw Molly's bright yellow car swing into town. He'd heard she was supposed to make it in on time for Dottie and Brady's wedding. Checking his watch, he saw she had three hours to spare. With the top down, hair waving in the wind, she looked like a woman on top of the world. But she wasn't alone. She had a giant green plant sticking up in the front seat. It was so big there was no way she could have transported it without the top being down on her convertible. And the backseat also had things piled in it.

He climbed into his truck, and drove the two hundred yards down through town to Adela's, pulling to a stop behind Molly's car. Finding out how her trip had gone was the neighborly thing to do. He couldn't very well drive on by without at least saying hello, even if seeing her and not being able to tell her how he felt was going to be hard.

"Bob!" she exclaimed when she jumped out of her car. She was dressed in soft gray slacks and a pale pink top that looked soft and shimmery against her apricot skin. She looked as fresh as the dew in April.

He didn't get out, didn't trust himself to get out, not with the way he wanted to put his arms around her and beg her not to move to New York. What kind of man would he be if he did that?

She stopped beside his door and laid her hand on his arm, which hung out the open window. "I'm glad you made it back. How did it go?" he managed.

She smiled, and her eyes sparkled like green glass in the afternoon sun. "It went perfect. Wonderful."

Bob's heart sank. He'd been praying that everything had gone the way she dreamed it would go, but he figured he was allowed a moment of grief for his loss. "I'm happy for you."

She was still smiling and looking at him as if she

had more to tell.

"So," he prompted, "when do you start?"

She dropped her hand to her hip and rocked back and forth on her heels, her smile turning mischievous. "I don't."

"What!" Anger, raw and electric flashed through him. Throwing open his door, he stepped from the truck, yanked off his Stetson and rammed a hand through his curls. Poor Molly, here she was smiling when he knew her heart was breaking. "They turned you down? They actually passed up the best opportunity they ever had?" He patted her shoulder. "Well, it's their loss. You'll get another opportunity and it will be outstanding. Your work is wonderful, anybody can see that. So you, you just hang in there. Don't give up on your dream, because it's going to happen—what are you laughing about?" She was hysterical. He'd thought she was putting on a brave front for him and here she was going into hysterics. Her shoulders were shaking hard and tears were seeping out of the edges of her happy eyes.

He looked closer. Her eyes were happy. "What's going on here? Did I miss something?"

She nodded. Getting control of her laughter, she wiped the dampness off her cheeks with her fingertips and took a deep breath. "I turned *them* down."

He frowned. "Are you crazy?"

She shook her head, grinning. "Thinking clearly for the first time in my life."

"But, Molly, you dreamed of this. You deserve it. You'll be wonderful at it."

She shook her head and her eyes mellowed softly, searching his face, like…like she'd missed him. Bob's heart kicked him in the ribs, which was becoming a habit around Molly, but it didn't hurt because he'd gone numb. He tossed his hat through the window of his truck so both his hands were free and leveled his gaze on her. "What have you done, Molly?"

"I changed my mind," she quipped.

"Molly—"

She stopped his words with her fingertips. "Listen, please. When I went to New York, I went to the top of the Empire State Building, just like in all those movies, you know, *Sleepless in Seattle* and *An Affair to Remember*. Except, instead of going there to meet up with my one true love, I went there to prove to myself that I didn't need anyone in my life to make me happy. I didn't understand it at first, but I figured it out. You see, I was standing there gripping that chain-link fence, staring through it at the most beautiful sparkling skyline I've ever seen, and it hit me that I've been hiding behind my writing as if it was a chain-link fence. I don't want to do that anymore."

"Molly." He reached to cup her head with his hand, running it gently down the silken strands until his hand cupped her shoulder. "It's in your blood. You've just had a case of stage fright. I have faith in you. Have faith in yourself and make it happen. Call them. They'll take you back."

"No, you don't get it. Haven't you known kids who dream when they grow up they're going to be lawyers or firefighters? Or cops, teachers—the list goes on, but when they're grown, they choose a different life path. Bob, I love you. I know I'm not the wife you've dreamed of. But look." She swung toward her car and pulled out several books on how to make a house a home. "If you compromise just a little and don't mind living with a writer…I can continue my freelancing and see where God leads me with it. I can do this, Bob. I can. Look I even bought a plant. I may kill it by tomorrow, but I've been talking to it all the way from Ranger."

Bob closed his eyes. She looked so sincere. She'd said she loved him. She loved him. He sucked in a deep breath. His ribs protested, but he sucked it in anyway, battling the emotions overtaking him.

"Bob, do you love me?"

Her words cut through the war raging inside him

and he met her questioning gaze. How could he let her do this?

"I have this feeling that you do."

"It's true, Molly, I love you so much. That's why I can't let you do this."

He watched the corners of her lips tilt upward into a slow, warm smile.

"I knew you loved me. I prayed you did."

"But, Molly, your dreams—"

"Are here, in Mule Hollow with you. Dreams don't make sense without someone to share them with. Oh, Bob, I don't want you to marry someone else. I wrote all those wonderful things about you because you spoke to my heart from the moment we met. My heart recognized you before I did. Marry *me,* Bob, and let's dream a little dream of our own."

That did it. With God on their side, Bob knew they could make this work. Renewed and humbled by God's love, he slowly took her in his arms, feeling complete as he drew her near. "How can I refuse an offer like that?" He touched his forehead against hers. "But only if you believe this—I will cherish you and support you in your dream and do everything in my power to make you as happy as you've made me." Lowering his lips to hers, he kissed her and felt the beat of her heart next to his. It was the most wonderful feeling in the world and one he would cherish for the rest of his life.

EPILOGUE

"You may kiss the bride."

Molly watched as Brady took Dottie in his arms and kissed his new wife. It brought tears to her eyes and she glanced up at Bob, who was sitting beside her. He was smiling at her. And her heart did a flip-flop. She was overwhelmed by the reality that she was about to plan her own wedding and begin her own love story. Standing at the top of the Empire State Building, when she'd bowed her head in prayer and prayed for clarity, she'd felt God's reassurance so distinctly that she'd stared out across the city at the millions of lights surrounding her and felt as if each represented a nod that she was at last going down the right path.

Earlier, when she'd stepped out of her car to find Bob standing there, she'd had no second thoughts. Her place was with Bob. Always and forever.

Why I chose to set the *Texas Matchmakers* series in the Texas Hill Country

I'm a central Texas gal, living in pure cowboy country between Dallas and Houston. But for *The Texas Matchmakers* series I needed an area that was more remote. After all, for these stories to work I needed the cowboys to have to travel over an hour to get to the nearest larger town. Cowboy's work most days from daybreak to dark, making socializing any distance away from the ranch hard to do. Therefore, I chose the beautiful, varied terrain of the far, outer edges of Hill Country where towns are spread out and ranch land is vast.

The hill country is also known for its massive blankets of Bluebonnets in the spring, its gorgeous sunsets and rocky rolling hills that enable visibility to go for miles….which worked perfectly for my series. There are also rivers and cool springs and creeks that weave through the terrain making perfect places to add a little romance to my books. But also, the dangers of flash flooding is always there, adding danger to the stories when I need it. For the setting of a book, the hill country is perfect.

If you ever visit my home state and are looking for an area made for a wonderful road trips—which I love! One of my favorite places and a must see is the Enchanted Rock. This granite dome is one of the largest in the United States. It's also one of my dad's favorite places which makes it even more special to me. I hope you enjoy the few photos of the area that I've chosen to share—there were just too many to choose from!

So there you have it, why I chose to place my series in this area. I hope you enjoy my vision of the area surrounding my tiny fictional town of Mule Hollow.

Interview with Debra Clopton on Writing Romance

1 – *Did you always know you wanted to write romance novels?*

No, it never crossed my mind that writing was a possibility! Not until the end of my senior year of high school when my English teacher, who loved my writing assignments, suggested I should be a writer. I loved to read romance, and was drawn to cute romantic movies—Doris Day, Audrey Hepburn-but *me* writing a book never crossed my mind. But once that seed was planted I knew writing romance was what I wanted to do.

2 – *As a romance writer what are your greatest goals?*

To write books that touch reader's hearts and help them smile. Writing romance, *Dream With Me, Cowboy* to be exact, helped me smile again during the darkest days of my life, after my first husband's sudden death. Immersing myself into a story gave me an escape that I needed at that time. My greatest joy is when a reader writes and lets me know that my little books helped them smile when they needed it most.

3 – *What was your motivation for this Texas Matchmakers series?*

I love fish out of water stories, spunky heroines out of their element, shaken up by amazing cowboy heroes—those inspire me and I wanted to have a place to explore those storylines. Also, I knew when I began plotting this series I wanted to show my love of small-town living. I wanted to give readers a new setting full of a loveable cast of friends to read about. And I had such fun creating this world.

4 – *Where does your inspiration usually come from?*

From everything! Movies, conversation, true stories I hear or read that intrigue me and make me wonder how it would feel to be in that persons shoes…that really draws me in. Triggers for my imagination are everywhere—character's pop into my head right in the midst of a conversation with someone or the first line of a story will come to me and intrigue me and I MUST find out what happens after that line. If I want to know then I assume my readers will want to know too. Life inspires me. People inspire me. God just created me to do this and inspiration is everywhere.

5 – What's your secret to creating a compelling romance?

I strive to entertain my readers through the entire story—I love to try and keep my readers awake at night! I create a strong connection between my hero and heroine and amp up the tension as I go. There must be laughter and issues of the heart mixed together—I love setting up the cute meet of a story putting the hero and heroine at odds and then throwing them together in a fun, entertaining way to draw the reader into the story. Conflict of the heart and exterior world must wrap together so that the reader is rooting for that first kiss and the resolutions they arrive at as they work together to solve the deeper issues and fall in love along the way.

6 – *What is the most valuable advice on writing you ever received?*

Write the next book! And that's what I'm always doing. Not just because readers want the next book but because I want to see where the series is going. I LOVE the process of a new blank page…the possibilities are endless and I cannot wait to discover what is waiting for me to type onto that page. Of course I love getting to The End too. You know…I just love the whole process.

7 – *Where can we find out more about you Debra Clopton?*

On my website: www.debraclopton.com, on Twitter and Facebook. You can also join my reader group on Facebook: Debra Clopton's Book Posse. I love to connect with readers wherever you may find me!

More Books in the Series

Texas Matchmaker Series
Dream With Me, Cowboy (Book 1)
Be My Love, Cowboy (Book 2)
This Heart's Yours, Cowboy (Book 3)
Hold Me, Cowboy (Book 4)
Be Mine, Cowboy (Book 5)
Operation: Married by Christmas (Book 6)
Cherish Me, Cowboy (Book 7)
Surprise Me, Cowboy (Book 8)
Serenade Me, Cowboy (Book 9)
Return To Me, Cowboy (Book 10)
Love Me, Cowboy (Book 11)
Ride With Me, Cowboy (Book 12)
Dance With Me, Cowboy (Book 13)

Check out Debra's Other Series
Star Gazer Inn of Corpus Christi Bay
Cowboys of Dew Drop, Texas
Cowboys of Ransom Creek
Sunset Bay Romance
Texas Brides & Bachelors
New Horizon Ranch Series
Turner Creek Ranch Series
Windswept Bay Series

About the Author

Debra Clopton is a USA Today bestselling & International bestselling author who has sold over 3.5 million books. She has published over 81 books under her name and her pen name of Hope Moore.

Under both names she writes clean & wholesome and inspirational, small town romances, especially with cowboys but also loves to sweep readers away with romances set on beautiful beaches surrounded by topaz water and romantic sunsets.

Her books now sell worldwide and are regulars on the Bestseller list in the United States and around the world. Debra is a multiple award-winning author, but of all her awards, it is her reader's praise she values most. If she can make someone smile and forget their worries for a few hours (or days when binge reading one of her series) then she's done her job and her heart is happy. She really loves hearing she kept a reader from doing the dishes or sleeping!

A sixth-generation Texan, Debra lives on a ranch in Texas with her husband surrounded by cattle, deer, very busy squirrels and hole digging wild hogs. She enjoys traveling and spending time with her family.

Visit Debra's website and sign up for her newsletter for updates at: www.debraclopton.com

Check out her Facebook at:
www.facebook.com/debra.clopton.5

Follow her on Instagram at: debraclopton_author

or contact her at debraclopton@ymail.com

Made in the USA
Middletown, DE
23 February 2025